"It wasn't my idea to call you. We don't want you here."

The shock of seeing Miriam Kauffman standing in front of him took Sheriff Nick Bradley aback, but he quickly hid his surprise. It had been eight years since he'd laid eyes on her. A lifetime ago.

"Good morning to you, too, Miriam."

She pressed her lips together in a tight, tense line. After all this time, she still wasn't any better at hiding her opinion of him. She looked ready to spit nails. Proof, if he needed it, that she hadn't forgiven him.

"This is why we called you." Amber gestured toward the basket.

"You called me here to see a new baby? Congratulations to whomever."

"Exactly," Miriam said.

"What am I missing?"

"It's more about what we are missing."

"And that is?" Nick demanded.

"A mother to go along with this baby."

Books by Patricia Davids

Love Inspired

His Bundle of Love
Love Thine Enemy
Prodigal Daughter
The Color of Courage
Military Daddy
A Matter of the Heart
A Military Match
A Family for Thanksgiving
*Katie's Redemption
*The Doctor's Blessing
*An Amish Christmas
*The Farmer Next Door
*The Christmas Quilt
*A Home for Hannah

*Brides of Amish Country

Love Inspired Suspense

A Cloud of Suspicion
Speed Trap

PATRICIA DAVIDS

After thirty-five years as a nurse, Pat has hung up her stethoscope to become a full-time writer. She enjoys spending her new free time visiting her grandchildren, doing some long-overdue yard work and traveling to research her story locations. She resides in Wichita, Kansas. Pat always enjoys hearing from her readers. You can visit her on the web at www.patriciadavids.com.

A Home for Hannah

Patricia Davids

Love Inspired

Recycling programs
for this product may
not exist in your area.

™ LOVE INSPIRED BOOKS

ISBN-13: 978-0-373-81636-1

A HOME FOR HANNAH

www.LoveInspiredBooks.com

Printed in U.S.A.

But we are bound to give thanks always to God for you, brethren beloved of the Lord, because God hath from the beginning chosen you to salvation through sanctification of the Spirit and belief of the truth.
—2 Thessalonians 2:13

In memory of Dave.
The one, the only, the love of my life.

Chapter One

"Bella, what's wrong with you?" Miriam Kauffman pulled her arm from beneath the quilt to squint at her watch. The glow-in-the-dark numbers read one forty-five in the morning. Her dog continued scratching frantically at the door to her bedroom.

Miriam slipped her arm back under the covers. "I'm not taking you out in the middle of the night. Forget it."

Her yellow Labrador-pointer mix had other ideas. Bella began whining and yipping as she scratched with renewed vigor.

Miriam was tempted to pull her pillow over her ears, but she wasn't the only person in the house. "Be quiet. You're going to wake Mother."

Bella's whining changed to a deep-throated bark. At eighty-five pounds, what Bella wanted Bella usually got. Giving up in exasperation, Miriam threw back her quilt.

Now that Bella had her owner's attention, she plopped on her haunches and waited, tongue lolling with doggy happiness. In the silence that followed, Miriam heard a new sound, the clip-clop of hoofbeats.

Miriam moved to her second-story bedroom window. In the bright moonlight, she saw an Amish buggy disappearing down the lane.

When she was at home in Medina, such a late-night visit would mean only one thing— a new Amish runaway had come seeking her help to transition into the outside world. But how would anyone know to find her in Hope Springs? Who in the area knew of her endeavors? She hadn't told anyone, and she was positive her mother wouldn't mention the fact.

Miriam pulled a warm cotton robe over her nightgown and grabbed a flashlight from the top of her dresser. She patted Bella's head. "Good girl. Good watchdog."

Guided by the bright circle of light, she made her way downstairs in the dark farmhouse to the front door. Bella came close on her heels. The second Miriam pulled open the door, the dog was out like a shot. Bella didn't have a mean bone in her body, but her exuberance and size could scare someone who didn't know her.

"Don't be frightened—she won't hurt you," Miriam called out quickly as she opened the door farther. She expected to find a terrified Amish teenager standing on her stoop, but the porch was empty. Bella was nosing a large basket on the bottom step.

Miriam swung her light in a wide arc. The farmyard was empty. Perhaps the runaway had changed his or her mind and returned home. If so, Miriam was glad. It was one thing to aid young Amish people who wanted to leave their unsympathetic families when she'd lived in another part of the state. It was an entirely different thing now that she was living under her Amish mother's roof. The last thing she wanted to do while she was in Hope Springs was to cause her mother further distress.

Bella lay down beside the basket and began whining. Miriam descended the steps. "What have you got there?"

Pushing the big dog aside, Miriam realized the basket held a quilt. Perhaps it was a meant as a gift for her mother. The middle of the night was certainly an odd time to deliver a package. She started to pick it up, but a tiny mewing sound made her stop. It sounded like a baby.

Miriam straightened. *There's no way someone left a baby on my doorstep.*

Bella licked Miriam's bare toes, sending a chill up her leg. She definitely wasn't dreaming. She took a few steps away from the porch to carefully scan the yard with her light. "If this is someone's idea of a prank, I'm not laughing."

Silence was the only reply. She waited, hoping it was indeed a joke and someone would step forward to fess up.

The full moon hung directly overhead, bathing the landscape in pale silvery light. A cool breeze swept past Miriam's cheeks carrying the loamy scent of spring. The grass beneath her bare feet was wet with dew and her toes grew colder by the second. She rested one bare foot on top of the other. No snickering prankster stepped out of the black shadows to claim credit for such an outrageous joke.

Turning back to the porch, she lifted the edge of the quilt and looked into the basket. Her hopes that the sounds came from a tape recorder or a kitten vanished when her light revealed the soft round face of an infant.

She gazed down the lane. The buggy was already out of sight. There was no way of knowing which direction the driver had taken when he or she reached the highway.

Why would they leave a baby with her? A chill that had nothing to do with the cold morning slipped down her spine. She didn't want to be responsible for this baby or any other infant. She refused to let her mind go to that dark place.

A simple phone call would bring a slew of

people to look after this child. It was, after all, a crime to abandon a baby. As a nurse, she was required by law to report this.

But that would mean facing Sheriff Nick Bradley.

"Miriam, what are you doing out there?" Her mother's frail voice came from inside the house.

Picking up the basket, Miriam carried it into the house and gently set it in the middle of the kitchen table. "Someone left a baby on our doorstep."

Her mother, dressed in a white flannel nightgown, shuffled over, leaning heavily on her cane. "A *boppli!* Are you joking?"

"*Nee, Mamm,* I'm not. It's a baby."

Miriam's first thought had been to call 9-1-1, until she remembered who the law was in Hope Springs. She'd cut off her right arm before she asked for his help. Who could she call?

Ada Kauffman came closer to the basket. "Did you see who left the child?"

"All I saw was a buggy driving away."

Ada's eyes widened with shock. "You think this is an Amish child?"

"I don't know what else to think."

Ada shook her head. "*Nee,* an Amish family would welcome a babe even if the mother was not married."

"Maybe the mother was too afraid or ashamed to tell her parents," Miriam suggested.

"If that is so, we must forgive her sins against *Gott* and against her child."

That was the Amish way—always forgive first—even before all the details were known. It was the one part of the Amish faith that Miriam couldn't comply with. Some things were unforgivable.

Miriam examined the basket. It was made of split wood woven into an oval shape with a flat bottom and handles on both sides. The wood was stained a pale fruitwood color with a band of dark green around the top for decoration. She'd seen similar ones for sale in shops that carried Amish handmade goods. The baby started to fuss. Miriam stared at her.

Her mother said, "Pick the child up, Miriam. They don't bite."

"I know that." Miriam scooped the little girl from the folds of the quilt and softly patted her back. The poor thing didn't even have a diaper to wear. Miriam's heart went out to their tiny, unexpected guest. Not everyone was ready to be a parent, but how would it feel to be the child who grew up knowing she'd been tossed away in a laundry basket?

Stroking the infant's soft, downy cap of hair, she felt the stirrings of maternal attachment.

She couldn't imagine leaving her child like this, alone in the darkness, depending on the kindness of strangers to care for it. Children were not to be discarded like unwanted trash.

Old shame and guilt flared in her heart. One child had been lost because of her inaction. This baby deserved better.

Putting aside her personal feelings, she called up the objective role she assumed when she was working. Carefully she laid the baby on the quilt again to examine it. As a nurse, her field of expertise was adult critical care, but she remembered enough of her maternal-child training to make sure the baby wasn't in distress.

Without a stethoscope to aid her, it was a cursory exam at best. The little girl had a lusty set of lungs and objected to being returned to her makeshift bed. Who could blame her?

Ada started toward the stairs. "A little sugar water may satisfy her until you can go to town when the store opens and stock up on formula and bottles. I have your baby things put away in the attic. I'll go get them. It's wonderful to have a child in the house again."

Miriam stared after her mother. "We can't keep her."

Ada turned back in surprise. "Of course we can. She was left with us."

"No! We need to find out who her mother is.

She has made a terrible mistake. We need to help her see that. We need to make this right."

Ada lifted one hand. "How will you do that?"

"I...I don't know. Maybe they left a note." Miriam quickly checked inside the basket, but found nothing.

"*Vel,* until someone return for her, this *boppli* needs a crib and diapers."

Miriam quickly tucked a corner of the quilt around the baby. "*Mamm,* come back here. You shouldn't go climbing around in the attic. You've only been out of the hospital a week."

A stormy frown creased her mother's brow but quickly vanished. "I'm stronger than you think."

That was a big part of her mother's problem. She didn't realize how sick she was. Miriam tried a different approach. "You have much more experience with babies than I do. You take her, and I'll go hunt for the stuff."

Her mother's frown changed into a smile. "*Ja,* it has been far too long since I've held such a tiny one. Why don't you bring me a clean towel to wrap her in first."

Miriam did as her mother asked. After swaddling the babe, Ada settled into the rocker in the corner of the kitchen with the infant in her arms. Softly she began humming an Amish lullaby. It was the first time in ages that Miriam had seen her mother look content, almost…happy. Miriam knew her mother longed for grandchildren. She also knew it was unlikely she would ever have any.

Ada smiled. "I remember the night you and Mark were born. Oh, what a snowstorm there was. Your *daed* took so long to come with the midwife that I was afraid she would be too late."

"But the midwife arrived in the nick of time." Miriam finished the story she'd heard dozens of times.

"*Ja*. Such a *goot,* quiet baby you were, but your brother, oh, how he hollered."

"Papa said it was because Mark wanted to be born first."

"He had no patience, that child." Ada began humming again, but her eyes glistened with unshed tears.

Miriam struggled with her own sadness whenever she spoke of her twin brother. Mark's death had changed everyone in the family, especially her, but the old story did spark an idea.

"*Mamm,* who is the local midwife?"

"Amber Bradley does most of the deliveries around Hope Springs."

"Bradley? Is she related to…him? Is he married to her?" Did he have a wife and children of his own? Thinking about him with a family caused an odd ache in her chest. Miriam had taken pains to avoid meeting him during her months in Hope Springs. She realized she knew almost nothing about his current life.

Ada said, "*Nee,* he's not wed. Amber may be a cousin. *Ja,* I'm sure I heard she was his cousin."

Nicolas Bradley was the sheriff, the man Miriam had loved with all her heart when she was eighteen and the man responsible for Mark's death. Would the midwife involve him? Miriam hesitated but quickly realized she had no choice. She didn't have any idea how to go about searching for the baby's mother. If Amber chose to notify Nick, Miriam would deal with it. She prayed for strength and wisdom to make the right decision.

"The midwife might have an idea who our mother is. She is certainly equipped to take care of a newborn. If nothing else, she will have a supply of formula and the equipment to make sure the baby is healthy."

Ada frowned at her daughter. "I have heard she is a good woman, but she is *Englisch,* an outsider. This is Amish business. We should not involve her."

"I'm no longer Amish, so it isn't strictly Amish business. Besides, she may feel like we do and want to keep this out of the courts. I'm going to call her."

"You know I don't like having that telephone in my house."

Her mother tolerated Miriam's *Englisch* ways, but she hated to allow them in her Amish home. It was a frequent source of conflict between the two women.

Irritated, but determined to remain calm, Miriam said, "I'm not giving up my cell phone. You are a diabetic who has already had two serious heart attacks. You could need an ambulance at any time. If you want me to stay, I keep the phone."

"I did not say you should leave. I said I do not like having the phone in my house. If I live or die, it is *Gottes wille* and not because you have a phone."

"It might be God's will that I carry a phone. Did you ever consider that?"

"I don't want to argue." Ada clamped her lips in a tight line signaling the end of the conversation.

Miriam crossed the room and dropped a kiss on her mother's brow. "Neither do I. I have said I'll only use the phone in an emergency and for work. I think this counts as an emergency."

When her mother didn't reply, Miriam quickly ran upstairs to her bedroom and pulled her cell phone from the pocket of her purse. A call to directory assistance yielded Amber Bradley's number.

When a sleepy woman's voice answered the phone, Miriam took a deep breath and hoped she was making the right decision. "Hi. You don't know me. My name is Miriam Kauffman, and I have a situation."

After Miriam explained what had transpired, Amber agreed to come check the baby and bring some newborn essentials. She also agreed to wait until they had discussed the situation before notifying the local law enforcement.

Miriam returned to the kitchen. Her mother was standing beside the kitchen table. She had taken the quilt out of the basket. Miriam said, "Amber Bradley is on her way. I convinced her to wait before calling the police, but I know she will. She has to."

Ada held up an envelope. "I told you not to involve the *Englisch*. I found a note under the quilt. The child's name is Hannah and her mother is coming back for her."

The farmhouse door swung open before Sheriff Nick Bradley could knock. A woman with fiery auburn hair and green eyes stood framed in the doorway glaring at him. "There has been a mistake. We don't need you here."

The shock of seeing Miriam Kauffman standing in front of him took him aback. He was certain his heart actually stopped for a moment before chugging ahead with a painful thump. He struggled to hide his surprise. It had been eight years since he'd laid eyes on her. A lifetime ago.

He touched the brim of his trooper's hat, determined to maintain a professional demeanor no matter what it cost him. How could she be more beautiful than he remembered? "Good morning to you, too, Miriam."

After all this time, she wasn't any better at hiding her opinion of him. She looked ready to spit nails. Proof, if he needed it, that she hadn't forgiven him. A physical ache filled his chest.

"Miriam, don't be rude," her mother chided from behind her. Miriam reluctantly stepped aside. A large yellow dog pushed past her and came out to investigate Nick's arrival. It took only a second for the dog to decide he was a friend. She jumped up and planted both front feet on his chest. He welcomed the chance to regain his composure and focused his attention on the dog.

"Bella, get down," Miriam scolded.

The dog paid her no mind. The mutt's tail wagged happily as Nick rumpled her ears. He said, "That's a good girl. Now down."

The dog dropped to all fours, then sat quietly

by his side. He nodded once to Miriam and entered the house. The dog stayed outside.

His cousin Amber sat at the kitchen table. "Hi, Nick. Thanks for coming. We do need your help."

Ada Kauffman sat across from her. A large woven basket sat on the table between them. The room was bathed in soft light from two kerosene lanterns hanging from hooks on the ceiling. The Amish religion forbade the use of electricity in the home.

He glanced at the three women facing him. Ada Kauffman was Amish, from the top of her white prayer bonnet on her gray hair to the tips of her bare toes poking out from beneath her plain, dark blue dress. Her daughter, Miriam, had never joined the church, choosing to leave before she was baptized. Tonight, she wore simple dark slacks and a green blouse that matched her eyes. Her arms were crossed over her chest. If looks could shrivel a man, he'd be two feet tall in about a second.

His cousin Amber wore jeans, sneakers and a blue T-shirt beneath a white lab coat. She served the Amish and non-Amish people of Hope Springs, Ohio, as a nurse midwife. Exactly what was she doing here? If Miriam's trim figure was anything to go by she didn't require the services of a midwife.

Amber wasn't normally the cloak-and-dagger type. He was intensely curious as to why she had insisted he come in person before she'd tell him the nature of the call.

He said, "Okay, I'm here. What's so sensitive that I had to come instead of sending one of my perfectly competent deputies? Make it snappy, Amber. I'm leaving in a few hours for a much-needed, week-long fishing trip, and I've got a lot to do."

"This is why we called you." Amber gestured toward the basket. He took a step closer and saw a baby swaddled in the folds of a blue quilt.

"You called me here to see a new baby? Congratulations to whomever."

"Exactly," Miriam said.

He looked at her closely. "What am I missing?"

Amber said, "It's more about what we are missing."

"And that is?" he demanded. Somebody had better start making sense.

Ada said, "A mother to go with this baby."

He shook his head. "You've lost me."

Miriam rolled her eyes. "I'm not surprised."

Her mother scowled at her, but said, "Some-one left this baby on my porch."

"Someone abandoned this infant? When? Did you see who it was?" He pulled his notebook and pen from his pocket and started laying out an investigation in his mind. So much for start-ing his vacation on time.

"About three hours ago," Miriam answered.

Was she serious? "And you didn't think to call my office until thirty minutes ago?"

Miriam didn't answer. She sat in a chair be-side his cousin. Amber said, "Miriam called me first. We've been discussing what to do."

"There is nothing to discuss. What you *do* is call your local law enforcement and report an abandoned child. We could have had a search for the parents started hours ago. Amber, what were you thinking? I need to get my crime scene people here. We need to dust for prints, collect evidence."

Miriam said, "No one has committed a crime."

He glared at her. "I beg to differ."

Her chin came up. She never was one to back down. He'd missed their arguments as much as he'd missed the good times they shared. If only they could go back to the way it had been before.

For a second, he thought he saw a softening in her eyes. Was she thinking about those golden summer days, too? Her gaze slid away from him before he could be sure. She said, "According to the Ohio Safe Haven Law, if a baby under one month of age is left at a fire station, with a law enforcement officer or with a health care worker, there can be no prosecution of the parents who left the child."

He didn't like having the law quoted to him. "This baby wasn't left with Amber or at a hospital. It was left with you."

"I'm a nurse."

She really enjoyed one-upping him. He had to admire her spunk. "But this isn't a hospital, it's a farmhouse. I still have to report this to the child welfare people. They will take charge of the baby."

"That's why we wanted to talk to you and not to one of your deputies." Amber had that wheedling tone in her voice. The one that had gotten him in trouble any number of times when they were kids.

Ada smiled brightly. "Would you like some coffee, Sheriff? A friend brought us cinnamon rolls yesterday. Perhaps you would enjoy a bite." She shuffled across the kitchen and began getting out plates.

The baby started to fuss. One tiny fist waved

defiantly through the air. Miriam stood and lifted the child out of the basket. She sat down in the rocker beside the table. Holding and patting the baby, she ignored him.

He exhaled the frustration building inside him. The Amish dealt with things in their own fashion and in their own time. He knew that. Miriam might not have been baptized into the faith, but she had been raised in it. Intimidation wasn't going to work on her or her mother.

He crouched in front of Miriam and took hold of the infant's waving fist. The baby grasped his finger and held on tight. It was a cute little thing with round cheeks and pale blond hair. He smiled. "Is it a boy or a girl?"

Miriam wouldn't meet his gaze. "A girl."

He looked at Amber. "Is she healthy? I mean, is she okay?"

"Perfectly okay," Amber assured him.

"How old do you think she is?"

"From the look of her umbilical cord, a day at the most."

He looked around the room. "What aren't you telling me?"

Miriam finally met his gaze. Perhaps it was a trick of the lamplight, but he didn't see anger in their depths. She said, "I saw an Amish buggy driving away."

He wasn't expecting that. To the Amish, faith

and family was the core around which everything was based. An abandoned Amish child was almost unheard of. It had never happened in his county.

"She's coming back for her child," Ada stated firmly.

Miriam stayed silent. She didn't take her eyes off the baby's face.

Amber laid a hand on Nick's shoulder. "The baby needs to be here when she does."

He rose to his feet and held up his hands. "Wait a minute. There are protocols in place for things like this. The child goes to the hospital to be checked out."

Miriam quickly said, "She's fine, but we'll take her into the clinic in Hope Springs for a checkup."

"Child Protective Services must place the baby with a licensed foster care provider or approved family member. I can't change that rule."

"I'm a licensed foster care provider," Miriam said and smiled for the first time. The sight did funny things to his insides. She should smile more often.

Surprised by a sudden rush of attraction, he struggled to regain his professionalism. "Good. Then you can offer your services to our child welfare people. If they agree, I don't see why you can't care for the baby. I would have brought a car seat with me if you'd told me I was coming to pick up a child. Now, I'll have to have someone bring one out. Unless you have one I can borrow, Amber?"

"I have one, but hear us out before you make a decision or call anyone else."

"I'm not breaking the law for you, cousin."

"Nor will you bend it, even if the outcome destroys a life." Miriam stood with the baby and moved away from him.

He'd been waiting for that. She knew exactly how to dig at the most painful part of their past. "Miriam, that's not fair. You know I would change things if I could."

"You can't. My brother is still dead."

"It was *Gottes wille,* Miriam. You must accept that. I forgave Nicolas long ago," her mother said quietly.

Miriam didn't reply. Nick knew a moment of pity for her. It couldn't be easy carrying such bitterness. It had taken him a long time to forgive himself for the crash that took her brother's life. With God's help, he had found the strength to accept what could not be changed and to live a better life because of it.

He caught Amber's questioning look. She had no idea what was going on. He shook his head and mouthed the word *later*. His history with the Kauffman family had no bearing on this case.

"What is it you want me to do?" he asked.

Amber said, "The mother left a note. She's coming back in a week. We feel that technically she hasn't abandoned her child. She simply left her with neighbors."

"Why am I here at all?" he asked.

Ada withdrew the note from her pocket and handed it to him. It was written on plain notebook paper.

Please help us. I know this isn't right, but I have no choice. It isn't safe to keep my baby right now, but I'll be back for her. Meet me here a week from tonight. If I can't make it, I'll come the following week on Friday at midnight. I love my baby with all my heart. I'm begging you to take care of her until I return. I pray God moves you to care for her as you would your own. Her name is Hannah.

Amber said, "We called you because it's clear this young woman is in trouble. We want you to help us find her."

He glanced at Miriam. She was expecting him to deny their request. He could see it in her eyes and in the set of her chin. No matter what

Miriam thought of him there was a woman in trouble and he couldn't ignore that. He said, "Ada, do you have a clean plastic bag?"

"Ja." She opened a cabinet door and withdrew a zip-top bag.

Nick said, "Hold it open for me." She did, and he slipped the note inside.

He glanced around at the women in the room. "What I think should happen is irrelevant. I have to uphold the law. I'm not sure if we have a crime here or not. I need to speak with the county attorney before I can let this child stay here."

Miriam glanced out the window for the umpteenth time. Dawn was spreading a blanket of rose-colored light across the eastern sky. Nick had spent the past twenty minutes sitting in his SUV. Now, he held his phone to his ear as he slowly paced back and forth on the porch. Bella sat watching him, her normal exuberance totally missing. Miriam found it hard to believe that Nick hadn't rejected their request outright and whisked Hannah into protective custody.

He owed no allegiance to the Amish. They didn't vote him into office or elect any officials. While they were a peaceful, quiet people, many *Englisch* saw them as an annoyance. Their buggies slowed traffic to a crawl and even caused accidents. Their iron horseshoes damaged the roadways for which they paid no motor vehicle taxes to maintain. They often owned the best farmland and rarely sold to anyone who wasn't Amish. Many outsiders looked down on them because they received only an eighth-grade education. They were outdated oddities in a rapidly changing, impatient world.

"What's taking him so long?" she muttered.

Amber spread a fluffy white towel on the table and laid the baby on it. From her case, she withdrew a disposable diaper and a container of baby wipes. "Nick understands what is needed. He respects the Amish in this community. He'll help us, you'll see."

Miriam found her eyes drawn to Nick once more. He made a striking figure silhouetted against the morning sky in his dark blue uniform. He'd always been handsome, but age had honed his boyish good looks into a rugged masculinity that was even more attractive. He'd gained a little bulk in the years since she'd seen him, but it looked to be all muscle. He was tall with broad shoulders and slim hips. At his waist he wore a broad belt loaded with the tools of his trade: a long black flashlight, a gun and handcuffs among other things.

As she watched, he raked his fingers through his short blond hair. She knew exactly how silky his hair felt beneath her fingertips. His hat lay on the counter beside her. She picked it up, noticing the masculine scent that clung to the felt. In an instant, she was transported back to the idyllic summer days they had enjoyed before her world crashed around her.

Thinking of all she had lost was too painful. Quickly she put the hat down and clasped her hands behind her back. "What is taking so long? Surely, he could make a decision by now. Either the baby can stay with us or she can't."

The outside door opened and Nick came in. He looked around the room until his gaze locked with Miriam's. She couldn't read the expression on his face. Was it good news or bad?

Chapter Two

"Well? What did you decide?" Amber demanded. "Do we have to involve social services?"

Nick couldn't take his eyes off Miriam. Emotions could cloud a man's judgment, and Miriam raised a whole bushel of emotions in him. She had since the first day they met when he was nineteen and she was an eighteen-year-old, fresh-faced, barefoot Amish beauty. Did she remember those wonderful summer days, or had her brother's death erased all the good memories of their past?

He brought his attention back to the present issue. "I've talked it over with the county attorney. He is willing to agree that the baby has not been abandoned, although the situation is certainly unusual. Hannah can remain in the custody of Ada and Miriam Kauffman for a period of seven days."

Miriam's eyes widened with surprise. "She can?"

"For *two* weeks," Amber said with a stubborn tilt of her chin.

Nodding curtly, Nick said, "However, if the family has not returned for her after two weeks, she becomes an abandoned infant, and I will call Child Protective Services."

"I'm sure someone will come forward before then." Amber's obvious relief eased some of his misgivings. She was more familiar with the Amish in the Hope Springs area than almost anyone. If she thought he was doing the right thing, he was willing to follow her recommendation.

Miriam didn't say another word. It was a struggle to keep from staring at her. He couldn't believe she still had such a profound effect on him. He had stopped seeing her the summer he turned twenty because he knew how strong her faith was and how important it was to her. He hadn't been willing to make her choose between her religion and his love.

The truth was he'd been afraid he would come out the loser. As it turned out, he had, only for a different reason.

He cleared his throat. "I've checked for reports of missing or abducted infants. Just because you saw an Amish buggy driving away doesn't automatically make this an Amish infant. Fortunately, there aren't any babies under one week of age that have gone missing nationwide. We'll go with your theory until there is evidence otherwise. If an infant girl is reported missing, that changes everything."

He paused. They weren't going to like the rest of what he had to say. "Now, I'm not willing to let someone who dropped a baby on your doorstep just waltz in and take her back. If they do show up, this will be immediately reported to Social Services."

Miriam glared at him. "I thought the point of us keeping the baby was to avoid that?"

"By letting you keep the baby, I'm making it easier for the mother to return or for her family to come forward when they might not do so otherwise. I'm sorry. I won't budge on this. Someone who is desperate enough to leave her child with you in the dead of night needs help—she needs counseling. I mean to see that she gets it."

The women exchanged looks. Ada and Miriam nodded. Nick breathed a mental sigh of relief. He said, "The note is too vague to open an official investigation into the mother's whereabouts. I see concern, but there is no evidence of a crime. 'It's not safe' could mean any number of things. However, I agree that we need to make an effort to find this young woman. The sooner, the better."

Amber threw her arms around him. "You're the best cousin I could ever ask for."

"That's not what you said when I wouldn't tear up your speeding ticket."

Amber blushed and cast a quick look at Miriam. "He's joking."

He rolled his eyes. "Right. Ladies, I don't want word of this baby getting out to the general public. Keep it in the Amish community and keep a lid on it."

Miriam frowned. "I would think public exposure is exactly what we want."

"When news of an abandoned baby surfaces, the nut cases come out of the woodwork. Women who desperately want children will claim it's their baby. Some are crazy enough that they will try to take legal action against you. People who want to adopt and simple do-gooders will come forward with offers to take the child. Trust me, it could become a media circus and a nightmare trying to sift fact from fiction."

"All right. Where do we start?" Amber asked.

"We can start by trying to tie the basket or the quilt to a specific family."

Ada spread the blanket open on the table so they could examine it. It was a simple quilt of patchwork blocks with a backing of blue-gray cotton. She said, "I don't see a signature or date, nor do I recognize the stitch work. It's fine work. Perhaps someone in the community will recognize it."

Nick put the basket on the quilt and snapped several pictures with his cell phone. "I'll email these photos to some of the shops that carry Amish goods. Maybe we'll get a hit that way."

Amber's cell phone rang. She opened it and walked away to speak to the caller.

"What else can we do?" Miriam asked.

"Do you recall what kind of buggy it was?"

"It was dark. I saw a shape, not much else."

"Did it have an orange triangle on the back, reflective tape or lights?"

"I couldn't tell."

"So we can't even rule out the Swartzentruber Amish families in this area. They don't use the slow-moving-vehicle signs. What about the horse? Could you recognize it again if you saw it?"

"No, I didn't see the animal, just the back of the buggy."

Amber returned to the room and said, "I'm sorry, but I've got to go. I have a patient in labor. Miriam, I'll leave the car seat with you. Nick, can you help me get it out of my car?"

"Sure." He followed his cousin outside to her

station wagon knowing she was going to grill him about his past relationship with Miriam.

Amber opened the door to the backseat. "It sounds like you have a history with the Kauffman family. Why don't I know about it?"

He leaned in to unbuckle the child safety seat. "It was years ago. You were away at school."

"Care to fill me in now?"

Lifting the seat out of the car, he set it on the roof and stared out across the fertile farmlands waiting for spring planting. He could hear cattle lowing in the distance and birds chirping in the trees. The tranquility of the scene was at odds with his memory of that long-ago night.

He closed his eyes. "The summer I turned nineteen, I started working for Mr. Kauffman as a farmhand. They lived over on the other side of Millersburg back then. It was our grandmother's idea. She thought I should learn how hard it was to work a farm the way the Amish do. She thought it would give me a better appreciation of the land."

"Grandmother is usually right," Amber said with a twinkle in her eye.

"She is. Anyway, I worked there for two summers. Miriam, her brother Mark and I became good friends."

"Why do I sense you and Miriam were more than friends?"

"We were kids. We fell in love with the idea of being in love, but she was strict, Old Order Amish. We both knew it wouldn't work. We chose to remain friends. It wasn't until a few years later that things changed."

"What happened?"

Nick took a stick of gum from his pocket using the added time to keep his emotions in check. Even now, it was hard to talk about that night. He popped the gum in his mouth, deftly folded the foil into a small star and dropped it back in his shirt pocket.

"Ten years ago I was a brand-new deputy and a bit of a hotshot back then. I didn't go looking for trouble, but I didn't mind if I found it. One night, we got a report of a stolen car. On the way to investigate, I caught sight of the vehicle and put on my lights. The driver didn't stop. Long story short, a high-speed chase ensued. A very dangerous chase."

"What else were you supposed to do?"

"Protocol leaves it up to the responding officer's discretion. What I should have done was drop back and stop pressing him when I saw the risks he was willing to take. I should have called for a roadblock to be set up ahead of us. I didn't do any of those things. I kept after the car. It was a challenge to outdrive him, and I wasn't about to back down."

"It sounds like you were doing the job you'd trained to do. I know your father was killed during a traffic stop. I'm sure that made you doubly suspicious of anyone who tried to get away."

She was right. "That did factor into my decision, but it shouldn't have. I tried to get around the car, but we slammed into each other. The other driver lost control and veered into a tree. I'll never forget the sight of that wreckage. The driver was killed instantly. It was Mark, Miriam's twin brother."

Amber laid a comforting hand on his shoulder. "I'm sorry. I didn't mean to make you relive the whole thing."

"You want to know the really ironic thing? I'm the one who taught Mark how to drive. I never understood why he didn't just stop. He'd never been in trouble. I doubt he would have spent more than one night in jail. To have his life ended by a *rumspringa* stunt, a joy ride, it wasn't right."

"The Amish believe everything that happens is God's will, Nick. They don't blame you. That would be against all that they hold sacred."

"Miriam blames me. I tried to talk to her after Mark's funeral. Even months later she wouldn't see me. As you can tell, her feelings haven't changed."

"Then she needs our prayers. Finding forgiveness is the only way to truly heal from such a tragedy."

He lifted the car seat from the roof of Amber's car. "You should get going. You don't want the stork to get there ahead of you."

Amber grinned. "You're still planning on coming to my wedding, right?"

"Rats, when was that again? I might be fishing."

She punched his arm. "A week from this coming Saturday and you'd better not stand me up for a trout."

"Ouch, that's assaulting an officer. I could arrest you for that."

"Whatever. Phillip would just break me out of jail."

"Are you sure of that?"

"Absolutely—almost sure. Tell Miriam she can bring the baby into our office anytime tomorrow morning. I happen to know Dr. White has a light schedule. If the baby begins to act sick before then, she should take her to the hospital right away. She's a nurse. She'll know what to do."

"I'll tell her."

Her expression became serious once more. "Nick, Miriam had to know when she called me that I would involve the law. She might not admit it, but I think she reached out to you."

Nick considered Amber's assertion as she drove away. What if she was right about Miriam's actions? What if she was reaching out to him? Could he risk the heartbreak all over again if she wasn't? He glanced toward the house. She had left her Amish faith. That barrier no longer stood between them, but the issue of Mark's death did.

Nick was about to start a week's vacation. If he left town now, he might never have another chance to heal the breach with Miriam. He wanted that, for both their sakes. In his heart, he knew there was a reason God had brought them together again.

He shook his head at his own foolishness. He was forgetting the most important part of this entire scenario. Somewhere there was a desperate woman who needed his help. She and her baby had to be his first priority.

Miriam decided to ignore Nick when he came into the kitchen again. He held a car seat in his hands. The kind that could easily be detached from the base and used as an infant carrier. He said, "Would you like me to put it in your car?"

"I'll get it later."

"Is there anything else you ladies need?"

"We're fine," Miriam said quickly, wanting

him out of her house. She'd forgotten how he dominated a room.

Ada spoke up. "Would you mind bringing the baby bed down from the attic for us?"

His eyes softened as he smiled at Ada. "Of course not."

"I'll get it later, *Mamm,* I'm sure the sheriff has other things to do."

"I've certainly got time to fetch the crib for your mother."

His cheerful reply grated on Miriam's nerves. She felt jumpy when he was near, as if her skin were too tight.

Her mother said, "*Goot.* Miriam, I'll take Hannah."

Miriam handed over the baby. Her mother smiled happily, then looked to the sheriff. "Nicolas, if you would give me the bottle warming on the stove, I'll feed her."

He lifted the bottle from the pan at the back of the stove. To Miriam's surprise, he tested it by shaking a few drops of formula on his wrist, and then handed it over.

Did he have children? Was that how he knew to make sure a baby's formula wasn't too hot? Had he been able to find happiness with someone else, the kind of happiness that eluded her?

He caught her staring when he turned and asked, "Which way to the attic?"

She all but bolted ahead of him up the stairs to the second floor. The attic was accessed by a pull-down panel in the ceiling of her bedroom. She rushed into the room, swept up her nightgown and the lingerie hanging from the open drawer of her bureau, stuffed everything inside and slammed it shut. She whirled around to see him standing in the doorway.

Her bed wasn't made. Papers and books were scattered across her desk. A romance novel lay open on her bedside table. The heat of a blush rushed to her face. For a second, she thought she saw a grin twitch at the corner of his lips. Her chin came up. "I wasn't expecting company in my bedroom today."

The heat of a blush flooded her face. She stuttered, "You know what I mean."

Stop talking. I sound like an idiot.

Nick pointed to the ceiling. "Is that the access?"

"Yes." She worked to appear calm and composed, cool even. It was hard when his nearness sent her pulse skyrocketing and made every nerve stand on end.

He crossed the room and reached the cord that hung down without any trouble. The long panel swung open and a set of steps came partway down. He unfolded them and tested their sturdiness, then started upward. When he vanished into the darkness above her, Miriam called up, "Shall I get a flashlight?"

A bright beam of light illuminated the rafters. "I've got one."

Of course he did. She'd noticed it earlier on his tool belt. Sheriff Nick Bradley seemed to be prepared for every contingency from checking baby formula to searching cobweb-filled corners. *Strong, levelheaded, dependable,* they were some of the words she had used to describe him to her Amish girlfriends so long ago. It seemed that he hadn't changed.

Miriam jerked her mind out of the past. This had to stop. She couldn't start mooning over Nick the way she had when she was a lovestruck teenager. Too much stood between them.

He leaned over the opening to look down at her. "Any idea where the baby bed is? There's a lot of stuff up here."

"No idea. If you can't find a crib in an attic, you're not much of a detective." Her words came out sounding sharper than she intended. She was angry with herself for letting him get under her skin.

The sound of a heavy object hitting the floor overhead made her jump. It was quickly followed by his voice. "Sorry. I don't think it broke."

She scowled upward. "What was that?"

"Just an old headboard."

"Great grandmother's cherrywood headboard, hand carved by my great-grandfather?"

"Could be." His voice was a shade weaker.

Miriam started up the steps. "Let me help before you bring the house down on our heads."

"It's tight up here."

"It might be for a six-foot moose," she muttered. She reached the top of the steps to find him holding out his hand to help her. Reluctantly, she accepted it and stepped up into the narrow open space beside him. They were inches apart. She wanted to jump backward but knew there was nothing but air behind her. It was hard to draw a breath. Her pulse skipped and skittered like a wild thing. She pulled her hand from his.

He said, "It's tight even for a five-foot-three fox."

She could hear the laughter under his words. Annoyed at his familiarity, she snapped, "It's not politically correct to call a woman a fox."

He cleared his throat. "I was referring to your red hair, Miriam. It's also not politically correct to call an officer of the law a moose."

Turning away, he banged his head on a kerosene lamp hanging from one of the rafters.

She slipped past him on the narrow aisle. "If the shoe fits… I think the baby stuff is down here."

Beneath the dim light coming through a dormer window, she spied a cradle piled high with old clothes and blankets. A wide-rimmed black hat and a straw hat sat atop the pile. She knew before she touched them that they had belonged to Mark.

Tenderly Miriam lifted the felt hat and covered her face with it. She breathed deeply, but no trace of her brother's scent remained. A band tightened around her heart until she thought it might break in two.

"Are they Mark's things?" Nick asked behind her.

She could only nod. Even after all these years, it was hard to accept that she would never see him again. He'd been her other half. She was incomplete without him. She could hear his laughter and see his face as clearly as if he were standing in front of her.

Nick lifted a stack of boxes and papers from the seat of a bentwood rocker and set them on the floor. He took the clothing and blankets from the cradle and laid them aside, leaving the flashlight on top of the pile. Picking up the cradle, he said, "I'll take this down. You can bring the baby clothes when you find them."

He didn't wait for her reply. When he was gone, she sat in the rocker and crushed her brother's hat against her chest as hot tears streamed down her face.

Nick descended the attic steps with the sound of Miriam's weeping ringing in his ears. He wanted to help, but he knew anything he offered in the way of comfort would be rejected. It hurt to know she still grieved so deeply.

After making his way down to the kitchen, he found Ada and the baby both asleep in the rocker. The bottle in Ada's slack hand dripped formula onto the floor. When he took it from her, she jerked awake, startling the baby who whimpered.

"Habe ich schlafe?" Ada peered at Nick with confusion in her eyes.

"Ja, Frau Kauffman. You fell asleep," he answered softly.

Childhood summers spent with his Amish grandmother and cousins had given him a decent understanding of the Amish language. While it was referred to as Pennsylvania Dutch, it was really Pennsylvania *Deitsh,* an old German dialect blended with English words into a language that was unique.

Ada sat up straighter and adjusted the baby in her arms. "Don't tell Miriam. She already worries about me too much."

"It will be our secret. Where shall I put the cradle?"

"Here beside me. I sleep downstairs now. Miriam insists on it. She doesn't want me climbing the stairs."

Taking a dishcloth from the sink, Nick mopped up the spilled milk. "I imagine Miriam gets her way."

Ada looked toward the stairs, then leaned closer to Nick. "Not so much. If I get well, she will leave again. I may be sickly all year."

He grinned. "That will be our secret, too."

"*Goot.* Where is she?"

Nick's grin faded. "She's still in the attic. She found some of Mark's things. I don't think she was ready for that."

"My poor daughter. She cannot see the blessings God has given her. She only sees what she has lost."

"She needs more time, that's all."

"No, it is more than that. I miss my son every day. I miss my husband, God rest his soul. I mourn them, but in God's own time I will join them in heaven. Until then, He has much for me to do here on earth. It will soon be time to plant my garden. With the weather getting nicer, I must visit the sick and the elderly. I have baking to do for the socials and weddings and I must pray for my child."

"I'll pray for her, too."

"Bless you, Nicolas. I accept that Miriam will never return to our Amish ways, but my child carries a heavy burden in her heart. One she refuses to share. I pray every day that she finds peace."

Ada struggled to her feet. Nick gave her a hand. "*Danki*. Take the baby, Nicolas."

"Sure." He accepted the tiny bundle from her amazed at how light the child was and how nice it felt to hold her.

"Sit. This cradle needs a good cleaning after more than twenty years in the attic. I'm so happy it is being put to use. It has been empty much too long."

Nick sat in the rocker and gave himself over to enjoying the moment. He hoped one day to have children of his own. Finding a woman to be their mother was proving to be his stumbling block.

He remembered how badly his mother had handled being a cop's wife. Even though he'd chosen small-town law enforcement over the big-city life his father craved, Nick wasn't eager to put a family into the kind of pressure cooker he knew his job could create. It would take a very special woman to share his life. Once, he'd hoped it would be Miriam, but that dream had died even before the wreck took her brother's life.

Chapter Three

Miriam had recovered her composure by the time she came downstairs. She saw Nick rocking Hannah while her mother was busy wiping down the dusty cradle. Miriam's eyes were drawn to the note still sitting in the plastic bag on the table. Somewhere, a young woman needed her help. She would concentrate on that and not on her tumultuous emotion.

She said, "It sounds like Hannah's mother is in an abusive relationship."

Nick said, "We're only guessing."

Miriam bit the corner of her lip. A young mother was having the worst day of her life. She'd done the unthinkable. She'd left her newborn baby on a doorstep. In her young eyes, the situation must have seemed desperate and hopeless. Miriam's heart went out to her. At least, she had chosen to give her child a chance. It was more than others had done.

Nick said, "The note raises questions in my mind about the mother's emotional state and about her situation but doesn't spell out a crime. I'll have it checked for fingerprints, but that's a long shot. If the person who wrote the note is Amish, I doubt we'll have his or her prints on file."

Miriam held up the bag to study the handwriting. "You think the father may have written this?"

"I think our mother had help. Do you believe a new mother could harness up the horse and buggy drive out here after she'd just given birth? That's one hardy woman if she did it alone."

Nodding, Miriam said, "You have a point."

Ada finished cleaning the cradle and covered the mattress with a clean quilt. "Amish women are tough. I know several who have had their child alone, and then driven to the home of a relative."

Nick handed the baby to Ada. "That may be, but I have to consider the possibility that she had help. Miriam, did you see which way the buggy turned after it reached the highway?"

"I'm sorry. I didn't." Miriam racked her memory of those few moments when the buggy had been in sight for something—anything that would help, but came up empty.

Somewhere a young woman needed help or she wouldn't have taken the drastic measure of leaving her baby on a doorstep. Miriam had spent too many hours with confused, frightened Amish teenagers not to know the signs. This was a deep cry for help. She had turned her back on one desperate mother years ago. Nothing but bitter ashes had flowed from that decision. She would not do it again. This time, she had to help.

Turning around, she grabbed her denim jacket from the peg by the door. "The lane is still muddy from the rain yesterday. We might be able to tell which way they turned."

"Good thinking." Nick pulled the door open and held it for her. Bella was waiting for them outside. She jumped up to greet Nick with muddy paws. He pushed her aside with a stern, "No." Bella complied.

Miriam glanced over her shoulder. "*Mamm,* it's time to check your blood sugar. This added stress and lack of sleep could easily throw it out of whack."

"All right, dear. I'll get the baby settled and I'll check it." She rocked the baby gently in her arms and cooed to her in Pennsylvania Dutch.

"You know what to do if it's low?"

"*Ja.* I'll have a glass of milk and recheck it in thirty minutes. The honey is in the cabinet if it is too low, but I feel fine. Stop worrying."

"I'll be back in a few minutes." Worrying was what Miriam did best these days. Her mother didn't seem to realize how precarious her health was.

Outside, Miriam walked beside Nick down the lane. He asked, "How long has your mother been ill?"

"She had her first heart attack seven months ago. That's when they discovered she was a diabetic. She had a second heart attack three weeks ago. Thankfully, it wasn't as bad as the first one. She's been doing okay, but I think she should be recovering more quickly than she has. Her energy level is so low. Everything makes her tired, and that frustrates her."

"You've been here in Hope Springs for seven months?" He seemed amazed.

"Yes." She'd taken pains to remain under his radar. Coming face-to-face with Nick was the last thing she wanted. His presence brought back all the pain and guilt she'd worked so hard to overcome. Now, he was in her home and in her business with no signs of leaving. Why hadn't she followed her mother's advice and left the midwife out of this?

"I imagine you had to quit your job in order

to stay this long." His sympathetic tone showed real compassion. It was hard to stay angry with him when he was being nice.

"I took a leave of absence from my job. My leave will be up in another month. I don't know what I'll do if I can't go back by then."

"That's got to be hard on both of you."

"She doesn't have anyone else." As soon as Miriam said it, she regretted pointing out the obvious.

A muscle in his jaw twitched, but his voice was neutral when he spoke. "We both know the Amish community will take care of Ada. She isn't alone."

"I know they will keep her fed and clothed, but she needs more than that. She needs someone to monitor her blood pressure and glucose levels and to make sure she takes her meds. She needs someone to make sure she eats the right things. If one more person drops by with a pan of cinnamon rolls or shoofly pie for her, I'm going to bar the door."

"Want to borrow my gun?" There was a hint of laughter in his tone.

"Don't tempt me," she replied, amazed that he could so easily coax a smile from her. Her anger slipped further away. They had both suffered a loss when Mark died, but their lives hadn't stopped. Nick had managed to move on. Perhaps she could, too.

He stopped and squatted on his heels to examine the ground. "My tires have erased any tracks the buggy might have left. I don't see anything distinctive about the horseshoe marks."

"Do you think the mother was coerced into leaving the baby?"

He rose and hooked his thumbs in his wide belt as he scanned the countryside. "Frankly, I don't know what to think. The whole thing doesn't fit. The Amish don't operate this way. It's so out of character."

"The Amish have flaws and secrets like everyone else." She would know. Flaws and secrets haunted her, every day and every night.

He must've heard something odd in her voice for he fixed her with an intense stare. She gazed at her feet.

He asked, "Who knows you are a nurse? Is it common knowledge?"

"I'm sure my mother has mentioned it to some of her friends."

"Did you notice the note said 'Meet me here a week from tonight.' Did that strike you as odd?"

"A little. Why?"

"I don't know. It just didn't seem to fit. What about someone from your past? An Amish friend who might know you're here with your mother."

"No, there's no one like that."

"How can you be so sure?"

"We were Swartzentruber Amish, remember? They are the strictest of the Old Order Amish. When I refused to join the faith, my parents had to shun me. My friends did the same. It wasn't until after my father died that my mother chose to become a member of a less rigid order."

"Didn't that mean she would be excommunicated by her old bishop?"

"Yes. She gave up her friends and the people she'd known all her life. It was very hard, but she did it so that she could see me again. She was accepted into Bishop Zook's congregation about a year ago. They are more progressive here. Unlike my old congregation, Bishop Zook's church believes a person has the right to choose the Amish faith. Those who don't are not punished."

He said, "Bishop Zook is not the only bishop who believes that. Amber's mother and my mother are sisters who both chose not to join the faith. They have siblings who remained Amish. My grandmother embraces all her family, Amish and English alike."

"Some districts are that way, some are more strict, some are rigid in their beliefs and don't tolerate any exceptions. People hear the word

Amish and they think the Plain People are all the same. There are enormous differences."

Miriam cocked her head to the side. "Wait a minute. If your mothers are sisters, why do you share the same last name with Amber?"

He grinned and started walking again, scanning the ground as he went. "Our mothers are sisters who married two brothers. Got to love small-town romances. Where did you live before you moved in with your mom?"

"Medina, Ohio."

Bella left Miriam's side and went hunting through the old corn stubble of the field beside them. It would soon be time for the farmer who rented her mother's land to begin planting new crops.

"What kind of nursing do you do?" Nick asked, slanting a curious glance her way.

Was he really interested? "I work in adult critical care."

"That's a tough job."

"Overdoses, strokes, trauma, heart attacks, we see it all."

"And car accidents." He looked away, but she saw the tension that came over him.

"Yes, car accidents," she replied softly.

She expected him to drop the subject, but to her surprise, he didn't. "Do you like it? I mean, not all the outcomes can be good."

"Every patient deserves the chance to reach their full potential. I'm part of a team that works to make that happen. Sometimes, what they regain isn't as much as they had before their event, but it's not for lack of trying on our part. For every loss of life, we see a dozen recoveries." It struck her as odd to be talking about her work with Nick, but she wanted him to know she was about making a difference in people's lives and she loved her work.

"When do you find the time to foster little kids?"

"I don't. I foster teens."

"Really?"

She met his gaze. There was a new respect in his eyes that she hadn't seen before. Lifting her chin, she said, "They are mostly Amish runaways."

He stopped in his tracks. "Today has been chock full of surprises."

"You don't approve? They are kids with nothing but an eighth-grade education. They don't have driver's licenses or social security cards. They are completely ill prepared for life in the outside world."

"I know that."

"If by some stroke of luck they can find work, they have to take low-paying jobs. Most get paid under the table from employers happy to take advantage of them. Without outside help, leaving the Amish is almost impossible for some of them."

"You left."

She started walking again. "Don't think it was easy."

"When did you start hating the Amish way of life?"

Stunned, she spun to face him. "I don't hate it. It's a beautiful way to live. The Amish believe in simplicity. Their lives are focused on faith in God and in keeping close family and community ties."

Quietly, he said, "They believe in forgiveness, too, Miriam."

"It sounds easy to say you forgive someone. Actually doing it is much harder. Did they ever catch the man who shot your father?"

He looked away. "No."

"It's tough when there's no justice in life, isn't it?"

Meeting her gaze, he nodded. "Yes. That's why I trust that God will be the ultimate judge of men."

She waited for the boiling anger to engulf her, but it didn't materialize. Maybe she was just too tired. She wanted to stay angry at him, but it was easier when she couldn't see the pain in his eyes. He knew what it was to lose someone he loved.

Nick started walking again. "If you admire the Amish, why help kids leave?"

"Because there are other ways to live that are just as important and as meaningful. You can't be a doctor or a nurse if you are Amish. You can't create new medicines or go to college, build dams or explore the oceans. You can't question the teachings of your church leaders. That said, two-thirds of the teenagers who come to me wanting a taste of *Englisch* life go back to their Amish families. Why? Because it's what they desire in their hearts. My job is to help them sort out what they truly want."

"Okay, I get it. That's cool." He walked to the edge of the highway and sank to his heels again as he examined the ground.

Did he get what she did and why? Or was he simply trying to placate her? She stopped a few feet away from him. Her shifting emotions made it difficult to stay focused on the task at hand.

He looked at her. "Could your efforts to help Amish youth be the reason someone brought this baby to you?"

"I don't think so. No one here knows what I do in Medina. My mother doesn't approve. While I'm living under her roof, I have to respect her feelings. Most people know me only as a driver for hire. I needed some kind of income while I'm here, and I can't spend the long hours away from Mom that a nursing job would require."

He gestured toward the road. "Our buggy went toward Hope Springs. See the way the impression of the wheels turn here and carried the mud out onto the highway."

"I do." She gazed at the thin tire track disappearing down the winding roadway. She could see half a dozen white Amish farmhouses along either side of the road before the road vanished over the hill. How many Amish families lived in that direction or on one of the many roads that branched off the highway? Fifty? A hundred? Where would they start looking for one scared, desperate young woman?

"Ah, now this is useful." Nick took a step closer to the roadway. A small puddle had formed after the rain. The imprint of the buggy wheel was deep where it rolled through the mud.

"What is it?" she asked.

He pointed to the print. "The buggy we are looking for has a jagged crack in the steel rim of the left rear wheel. If it breaks all the way through, someone is going to need a new rim put on."

"It looks like a crooked Z. It should be easy enough to spot."

He stood and rubbed a hand over his jaw. He took another stick of gum from his pocket, unwrapped it and popped it into his mouth. Carefully he folded the silver foil into a star. He noticed her stare and said, "I quit smoking a few years ago, but I can't kick the gum habit."

He had his share of struggles like everyone else. It made him more human. Something she wasn't prepared to see.

She looked away and asked, "How do we begin searching for Hannah's mother?"

"Even if I had the manpower to launch a full-scale investigation, I couldn't check every buggy wheel in the district. Most Amish families have three or four buggies, depending on how many of their kids are old enough to drive. It could take months."

"And Hannah has only two weeks before her mother's rights are severed if she doesn't return."

"Time may not be on her side."

"That's it? You're going to give up before we've started? I'm sorry I let Amber call you. I can tell you aren't going to go out of your way to save this family. I don't know why I thought you would."

Nick studied the myriad expressions that crossed Miriam's face and wondered where such passion came from.

He said, "I'm not sure I know what you want me to do?"

"We have a letter asking for help. We can't ignore it. This young girl's life may be ruined by a rash decision. I don't think we should wait for her to come back. I think we should go find her."

"Is there something you aren't telling me?"

It was as if his question had caused a mask to fall over her face. Her expression went completely neutral. Instead of answering his question, she said meekly, "I want to help, that's all."

Miriam's abrupt switch triggered his cop radar. She was hiding something. By her own admission few people knew she was a nurse. Fewer still would know that she aided Amish youth looking to leave their faith and go out into the world. Was accepting an unwanted baby part of her plan to help an unwed Amish girl escape into the *Englisch* life?

He didn't want to believe she would lie to him, but did he really know her? They hadn't spoken in years. People changed.

Maybe it wasn't a coincidence that Hannah had been left on Miriam's doorstep. If the mother knew Miriam, would she be able to stay away? He figured she would need to know how her little girl was doing. The sight of Miriam with the child just might draw that woman out if she were still in the Hope Springs area. He wanted to be around when that happened. It would mean spending time, lots of time, in Miriam's company.

Could he keep his mind on his job when she was near? At the moment, all he wanted to do was run his fingers through her gorgeous hair. The early morning sun brought fiery highlights to life in her red-gold, shoulder-length mane as it moved like a dense curtain around her face and neck. It was the first time he'd seen her without the white bonnet the Amish called a prayer *kapp*. In his youth, he'd fantasized about what her hair would look like down. His imaginings paled in comparison to the beauty he beheld at the moment.

He realized he was staring when she scowled at him. Forcing his mind back to the task at hand, he asked, "Are you sure you can't think of anyone who might be Hannah's mother? Maybe you gave a ride to her or to her family recently and mentioned you were a nurse."

"No one stands out. Believe me, I've been racking my brain trying to think who she might be."

"I need to get back to the office and have our note and the hamper run for prints. Why don't you make up a list of the families who might know you're a nurse? We can go over them later.

Something may click in the meantime. If it does, give me a call."

They returned to the house, covering the quarter mile in silence. When they reached his SUV, Miriam whistled for the dog. As Bella ambled up, she stopped to give Nick a parting lick on the hand. He patted her side. "She's a nice dog."

"Thank you."

"When did you rescue her from the pound?"

Miriam paused. "How did you know that?"

"It seems to be your MO."

"My what?"

"Your modus operandi, your mode of operation. Runaway teens, sick people, foundling babies—it just makes sense that your dog would be a rescue, too."

Her frown turned to a fierce scowl. "Don't think you know me, Nick Bradley, because you don't. You don't know me at all."

She turned on her heels and marched toward the house.

At the porch, she stopped and looked back. "My mother was right. This is Amish business. We will handle it ourselves. Have a great vacation."

Chapter Four

Miriam stopped short of slamming the door when she entered the house. Nick infuriated her. How dare that man presume to know anything about her? She didn't want him to know anything about her. She didn't want him to read her so easily.

She was scared of the way it made her feel. Like she could depend on him.

She balled her fingers into fists. She couldn't decide if she was angrier with him, or with herself. For a few minutes, she had forgotten what lay between. Somehow, after everything that happened, Nick still had the power to turn her inside out, as he'd done when she was eighteen and a naive country girl.

Well, she wasn't a teenager anymore. She wouldn't fall under his spell again. She had too much sense for that. There was too much that stood between them.

How could she have forgotten that even for a second? She had gone months without running into him. Why now? How much more complicated could her life get? Perhaps in the back of her mind she knew this would happen. That Nick would use his charm to make her forget her anger and forgive him.

If she forgave Nick, she would have only herself left to blame for Mark's death. She was the one who had sent her brother on his panicked flight that night. The guilt still ate at her soul. If only she'd had the chance to beg Mark's forgiveness, perhaps she could learn to live with what she'd done.

When Mark's *Englisch* girlfriend, Natalie Perry, had come begging for a word with him, Miriam had been only too happy to inform her Mark wasn't home. When the tearful girl explained that her parents were making her leave town the following evening, Miriam had been relieved. It was God's will. Without this woman's influence, her brother would give up worldly things and be baptized into the faith. Miriam had given up Nick's love for her faith. She had passed that test. Mark would, too.

Natalie had scrawled a note and pressed it into Miriam's hand, pleading with her to give it to Mark as soon as possible. At the time, Miriam had no idea what the note contained, but she didn't give it to Mark until late the next day. Only afterward did she understand what harm she had caused.

Mark had flown out of the house, stolen a car and tried to reach his love before it was too late. Nick had stopped him, and Miriam never had the chance to beg her brother's forgiveness.

The front door opened, and Nick came in looking as if he expected a frying pan to come sailing at his head. The idea of doing something so outrageous made her feel better. Slightly.

When he saw that he didn't need to defend himself, he said, "Ada, is there anything you need me to do before I leave? I can chop some kindling if you need it."

"*Nee,* I reckon we'll be fine."

He nodded. "You let me know if you hear anything from the baby's family."

Ada nodded toward the baby sleeping in the newly washed bassinet. "Do not worry, Nicolas. The mother, she will come for her babe."

"I pray you are right. Miriam, I'd appreciate knowing what the doctor has to say about Hannah."

He waited, as if he expected Miriam to say something. When she didn't, he nodded in her direction. "Okay, I've got to get back to town."

When the door closed behind him, Miriam

took the first deep breath she managed to draw all morning. "I thought he would never leave."

"It was *goot* to see him again. I remember him as such a nice boy."

"It's too bad he turned out to be a murderer."

"Do not say such a thing, Miriam!" Her mother rounded on her with such intensity that Miriam was left speechless.

Ada shook her finger at her daughter. "You are not the only one who has suffered, but you are the only one who has not forgiven. The more you pick at a wound, the longer it takes to heal. I don't know why you refuse to see that. I'm tired of your selfish attitude. Maybe it is best that you go back to your *Englisch* home."

Dumbfounded, Miriam stared at her mother in shock. Not once in her life had her mother raised her voice in such a manner.

Miriam struggled to muster her indignation. "That man caused the death of your only son. Have you really forgiven him for that?"

"It was *Gottes wille* that Mark died. I can't pretend to understand why such a thing had to happen, or why your father was taken before me, too. I can only try to live a good life and know that I will be with them when it is my time." Ada turned her back on her daughter and began to wash the coffee cups in the sink.

Miriam's anger slipped away. She wanted to punish Nick, but she'd wound up hurting her mother instead. "Do you really want me to leave?"

Her mother seemed to shrink before her eyes. Ada heaved a deep sigh. "I want what I cannot have. I'm tired. I'm going to lie down for a while. Can you watch the baby?"

"Of course." Miriam fetched her mother's cane from beside the table and watched her head toward the hallway. Ada moved slowly, leaning heavily on her cane for support.

Overcome with guilt, Miriam said, "I'm sorry if I upset you."

Her mother paused at the doorway and looked over her shoulder. "I forgave you the moment you spoke. We will talk no more about your stubborn, willful ways and the bitterness you carry. I leave it up to *Gott* to change your heart."

After her mother disappeared into her room Miriam sat down beside Hannah. Bella had staked out her new territory beneath the crib. She looked up at Miriam with soulful eyes and gave a halfhearted wag of her tail.

Miriam leaned down to pet her. "You love me no matter what I do or say. Thank you. That's why I have a dog."

* * *

The following morning, Miriam sat in the waiting room of the Hope Springs Medical clinic with Hannah in her borrowed car seat on the floor beside her. They were waiting to be seen for Hannah's first well-baby appointment.

Miriam was starting to wonder if she *was* a well baby. How soon did colic set in? If Hannah wasn't sick, she was certainly a fussy baby. It had been a long night for both of them. Miriam's eyes burned with lack of sleep. A headache nagged at the base of her neck. The baby had fallen asleep in the car on the way to the clinic, but she was starting to fidget now that the car ride was over.

"The doctor will be with you shortly. Would you like some tea or coffee while you wait?" Wilma Nolan, the elderly receptionist asked with an encouraging smile.

Miriam shook her head. What she wanted was a few hours of uninterrupted sleep. The outside door opened. She looked over and saw Nick walk in.

He was out of uniform this morning. He'd traded his dark blues for worn, faded jeans, Western boots and a wool sweater in a soft taupe color that made his tan look even deeper. No one could deny he was a good-looking man.

She struggled to ignore the sudden jump in her pulse.

The elderly receptionist behind the counter sat up straight and smiled. "Sheriff, how nice to see you. I'm afraid you will have quite a wait if you need to see the doctor this morning. Dr. White isn't feeling well, and Dr. Zook is the only one seeing patients."

"Not to worry, Wilma, I'm not sick. I just came to check on Ms. Kauffman and...the baby."

Wilma's eyebrows shot up a good two inches as she glanced between Miriam and Nick. "I see. Is this official business?"

Mortified by what she knew the receptionist was thinking, Miriam wanted to sink through the floor. Nick obviously came to the same conclusion because he quickly stuttered, "It's...it's personal business, Wilma."

"Oh, of course." A smug, knowing smile twitched on her thin lips as she blushed a bright shade of pink.

Nick took a seat beside Miriam. "Hi."

"What are you doing here?" she snapped under her breath, keeping a bland smile on her face for Wilma's benefit.

He leaned down to gaze at Hannah in her carrier. "I wanted to make sure she is okay. Amish babies have a higher incidence of birth defects, you know."

"Of course I know that. I thought you were going to wait for me to call you with an update."

"I wasn't sure you would call me."

He was right. She had no intention of involving him any more than she absolutely had to. "You didn't have to come in person. You know what Mrs. Nolan is thinking, don't you?"

"I'm not responsible for what people think."

"'It's personal business, Wilma.' Oh, you're *so* going to be responsible if word gets out that *we* are a couple with a new baby."

Nick shifted uncomfortably in his chair. "She's known me for years. We go to the same church. Even if she thought it, she would never repeat it to anyone."

"Hannah Kauffman?" A young man with thick-rimmed black glasses stood at the entrance to the hallway. He had two pens in the top pocket of his lab coat and a manila folder in his hands.

"It's not Kauffman, Dr. Zook," Nick stated as he picked up Hannah's carrier and walked toward the young doctor.

Miriam took the carrier away from Nick. "It is for now."

The doctor turned and walked down the hall

ahead of them. "Let us know what you put on the birth certificate and that will be her legal name."

"Legally, she's a Jane Doe." Nick stood close behind Miriam. The warmth of his breath on the back of her neck sent shivers rippling across her skin."

Dr. Zook stopped and looked at him in surprise. "She's a foundling?"

Miriam nodded. "Someone left her on my mother's doorstep two nights ago. I caught a glimpse of a buggy going down the lane. A note said her name was Hannah, but that's about all."

"I see now why you are involved, Sheriff. This is very odd."

Nick said, "I'm hoping you can help us."

Dr. Zook's eyes narrowed behind his glasses. "You do understand that I can't reveal any information about my patients."

"Even if you think you know who the mother might be?" Nick asked in a tone of voice that made Miriam glad she wasn't the one he was questioning.

Dr. Zook drew himself up to his full height, which was a good four inches shorter than Nick's six feet. "Not even then."

Miriam expected this roadblock. "I'm a nurse, so I understand how it works. We won't ask for confidential information."

The young doctor relaxed. "Good. Let's take a look at this little girl and make sure she is healthy."

He held open the door to an exam room. Miriam walked in and set the carrier on the exam table. Carefully, she unlatched the harness and lifted the baby out. Hannah began fussing but soon settled back to sleep as Miriam soothed her with rocking and quiet words.

Nick took the carrier and put in on the floor, making room for Miriam to lay the baby on the exam table. She took a step to the side, but kept one hand on Hannah. Dr. Zook quietly and thoroughly went about his examination.

Miriam had met him a few times before. She preferred Dr. Harold White, but the older physician was well into his eighties. Dr. Zook had taken over a small part of Dr. White's practice, and his involvement had grown in the past year until he oversaw almost half of the patients.

Miriam had been impressed with his handling of her mother's health issues and had no qualms about letting him see Hannah. She said, "I've always meant to ask, are you related to our Bishop Zook?"

The young doctor smiled. "All Zooks are related in one way or another, but in the case of Bishop Zook and myself, it's not a close connection. My family comes from near Reading, Pennsylvania."

Nick spoke up. "Can you tell if Hannah has any birth defects associated with being Amish?"

"I can rule out dwarfism and Troyer Syndrome, which is a lethal microcephaly or small head, and several others diseases just by looking at her. Only blood tests or time will tell us if she suffers from any inherited metabolic defects such as glutaric aciduria, PKU, maple syrup urine disease or cystic fibrosis. I'll draw her newborn screening blood tests today. That will check for many of the things I've mentioned and more. Do you want me to draw blood for DNA matching, as well?"

Nodding, Nick said, "You read my mind. If someone shows up claiming to be her parent or grandparent, I want to make sure they are related before I release her."

Miriam said, "The mother's note did say she would be back for Hannah, but she also said it wasn't safe to have the baby with her. Can you think of anyone in a situation like that?"

The doctor rubbed the back of his neck. "I honestly can't."

Miriam laid a hand on his arm. "I know the Amish are reluctant to go to outsiders with their problems, Doctor. If you hear of anyone in a difficult situation, please let us know."

Dr. Zook stared at her hand. She withdrew it hoping she hadn't made a mistake.

He looked into her eyes and said, "I do understand the reluctance of the Amish to become involved with Social Services and the legal system in general. They have not always been treated fairly. I respect the way they take care of each other. I deeply admire their faith in God. I will let you know if I hear of anything like this."

Miriam blew out a sigh of relief. "Thank you, Doctor."

"Not at all." He was actually blushing.

Nick gave Miriam a funny look, then said, "Thanks, Doc."

"I'll draw some blood for those tests and I'll have Amber follow up with this little girl just as she would one of her home deliveries. If you have any questions, feel free to call me. Day or night."

He took a card from his pocket and scrawled a number on it. He handed it to Miriam. "This is my personal cell phone. Don't hesitate to use it."

She smiled at him. "I won't hesitate for a minute."

"Is there anything else?"

Miriam said, "She's very fussy, Doctor, especially after she eats. I'm wondering if I should switch her to a soy-based formula."

"You can certainly try that, but don't make an

abrupt switch. Mix the two together a few times until you gradually have all soy in her bottles."

"All right. We'll try that."

"Fine. I'd like to see her again in two weeks. Sooner, if you have any concerns," he added.

When the appointment ended, Nick scooped up Hannah's carrier and held the door open for the doctor and Miriam to go out ahead of him. Outside the clinic, he handed the baby over to Miriam. She opened her rear car door and leaned in to secure the carrier.

He knew he shouldn't say anything, but as usual, his good sense went missing where Miriam was concerned. "Doctor Zook seems quite taken with you."

She popped up to gape at him. "What has that got to do with anything?"

"Nothing. It was a simple observation. I assume he isn't married?"

"No, he isn't, and I'm sure that is none of your business."

He liked the way her eyes snapped when she was angry. If only her anger wasn't always directed at him. He took a step back and raised his hands. "Don't get all huffy."

"I have every right to get huffy. What if I suggested Wilma had a crush on you?"

"Since she is old enough to be my grandmother, I'd say that would be weird."

"There's no talking to you. Now that you've been reassured Hannah is in good health, please go away. The less I see of you the better."

He hid how much her words hurt and gave her an offhand salute. "As you wish."

She rolled her eyes and turned her back on him to finish fastening Hannah's car seat. She struggled to get the last buckle fastened.

He didn't want to leave on a sour note, but he knew when he was butting his head against a brick wall where she was concerned. In spite of his best intentions, he couldn't help making one parting comment. "That chip on your shoulder isn't doing you any good, you know."

She backed out of the car with a growl of exasperation. He nudged her aside, leaned in and deftly secured the baby. Straightening, he looked at Miriam and calmly said, "It isn't going to do Hannah any good, either. We have a better chance of finding her mother if we work together."

"I thought you were leaving town for a fishing trip?"

He gazed at her intently. "The fish can wait. Hannah shouldn't have to."

He wanted Miriam's cooperation. He didn't believe in coincidences, he still believed whoever left the baby with her knew she was a nurse. "Did you put together the list of families who know you're a nurse, the way I asked?"

"Yes." She dug into her purse and pulled out a handwritten sheet.

It was a short list. There were only seven names on it. It wouldn't take long to interview these families. He looked at her. "I appreciate your cooperation."

Miriam considered carefully before she spoke again. If Hannah's mother didn't come forward, there would be little she could do on her own to find her. Nick, on the other hand, had an entire crime-solving department at his beck and call. If he was willing to put some effort into finding the baby's mother, Miriam shouldn't be discouraging him. In the end, finding the young woman who needed her help took priority over her feelings for cooperating with Nick.

She said, "I have an idea how we can check lots of buggy tires in one place."

He looked at her sharply. "How?"

"The day after tomorrow, Sunday preaching services will be held at Bishop Zook's farm. Every family in his congregation will be there. Including all the people on that list. The younger men usually drive separately so they can escort their special girls home afterward. Why go farm to farm when there will be dozens of buggies in one place? It's a start."

"A good start. Still, his isn't the only Amish church in the area. I can think of at least five others. I can try to find out where the other congregations are meeting. Tuesday is market day. That will be another opportunity for us if she hasn't come forward by then."

The thought of working with Nick should have left Miriam cold, but it didn't. Instead, a strange excitement quickened her pulse. What was she getting herself into?

"I'll see you Sunday," he said and walked away.

When he reached his vehicle, he glanced back. She was still standing by her car watching him. An odd look of yearning crossed his face. It was gone so quickly she wondered if she imagined it.

What was he thinking when he gazed at her like that? Was he remembering happier days? She licked her lips and tucked her hair into place behind her ear. Did he think she had changed much? Did he still find her attractive?

The absurdness of the thought startled her. Why should she care what he saw when he looked at her? Impressing him should be the last thing on her mind. She walked around her car, got in quickly and drove away.

But no matter how fast she drove, thoughts of Nick stuck in her mind. She couldn't out-run them.

Chapter Five

Sunday morning dawned bright and clear. Miriam knew that because her mother was clanging pots and pans around in the kitchen before any light crept through Miriam's window. The sounds echoed up the stairwell into her room because she had the door open to hear Hannah when she cried. She needn't have bothered. Each time the baby fussed, Bella was beside Miriam's bed five seconds later, nosing her mistress to get up.

Miriam's mother had put a cot in the kitchen to sleep beside the baby's crib, but Miriam had been the one to get up and feed the baby through the night. Her mother's intentions were good, but she needed her sleep, too. Tonight, Miriam would insist on taking the cot. That way she might get a little more sleep.

The soft sound of her mother humming

reached Miriam's ears. Ada was delighted her daughter was taking her to the Sunday preaching. Her mother might say she accepted that Miriam had left the Amish faith for good, but for Ada, that door was always open. Any former Amish who sought forgiveness would be welcomed back into the Amish fold with great joy.

Her mother hollered up the stairs. "You should feed the horse, Miriam. She will have a long day."

Miriam groaned. Arriving at a church meeting in a car was unacceptable to Ada. Amish people walked or drove their buggies. End of discussion.

To keep her mother from trying to walk the six miles to Bishop Zook's farm, Miriam would have to feed, water and hitch up their horse. She might be out of practice at harnessing the mare, but she hadn't forgotten how to do it.

After dressing in work clothes, Miriam walked through the kitchen. At the front door, she waited for Bella to join her. "Come on, the baby's not going to wake up for another two hours. I just fed her. This might be your only chance to spend time with me today because you are not coming with us to church."

Bella reluctantly abandoned her post beneath the crib and trotted out the door Miriam held open. Her mother, looking brighter than Miriam had seen her in weeks, was mixing batter in a large bowl. "You'd best get a move on, child. I'll not be late to services at the bishop's home. Esther Zook would never let me live it down."

"I can't understand why such a sweet man married that sour-faced woman."

Ada chuckled, then struggled to keep a straight face. "It is not right to speak ill of others."

"The truth is not ill, *Mamm,* it is the truth. There is only one reason I can think of why he fell for her."

The two women looked at each other, and both said, "She's must be a wondrous *goot* cook!"

Laughing, Ada turned back to the stove. "How many times did your father say those very words?"

"Every time he talked about his brother's wife, Aunt Mae."

"She was a homely woman, God rest her soul, but your *onkel* was a happy man married to her." Ada spooned the batter into a muffin tin.

Miriam's smile faded. "I miss Papa. He was a funny fellow."

"*Ja.* He often made me laugh. God gave him a fine wit. You had better hurry and get the horse fed or these muffins will be cold by the time you get back." Ada opened the oven door and slid the pan in.

Miriam walked outside into the cool air. Even after six months, she was still amazed by the stillness and freshness of a country morning. She scanned the lane for any sign of a returning buggy. It remained as empty as it had all night. She knew because she'd looked out her window often enough. Perhaps Hannah's mother wouldn't return. What would become of the baby then?

Had Nick had any luck lifting fingerprints from the note or hamper? Surely, he would have called if he had. She still found it hard to believe that he had agreed to leave the baby with them. Was he trying to make amends? Did he care that she hadn't forgiven him?

Annoyed with herself for thinking about Nick once again, she hurried across the yard to finish her chores. In the barn, she quickly measured grain for the horse and took an old coffee can full to the henhouse. Opening the screen door, she sprinkled the grain for the brown-and-white-speckled hens. They clucked and cackled with satisfaction. She didn't bother checking for eggs. She knew her mother had gathered them already.

By the time she returned to the house, hung up her jacket and washed up, her mother was dumping golden brown cornmeal muffins into a woven wooden basket lined with a white napkin. The smell of bacon filled the air and made Miriam's stomach growl. A few more years of eating like this and she would be having her own heart attack.

"What was your blood sugar this morning?" Miriam snatched a muffin and bit into the warm crumbly goodness.

"104."

Miriam fixed her mother with an unwavering stare. "Have you taken your medicine?"

"Ja."

"Checked your blood pressure?"

"Ja."

"What is your blood pressure this morning?"

Ada's eyes narrowed. "Before or after my daughter began badgering me?"

Miriam didn't blink. "Before."

Ada rolled her eyes. "110 over 66, satisfied?"

Smiling broadly, Miriam nodded. *"Ja, Mamm dat* is very *goot."*

"And we will be very late if you don't hurry up and eat." Her mother carried the empty muffin tin to the sink and then returned to the table. After bowing their heads in silent prayer, the woman began eating.

Ada asked, "Have you decided what to tell people about Hannah?"

"The truth is generally best. I will tell people she was left with us to care for until her mother returns."

The baby began to fuss. Miriam reached over to her cradle, patted her back and adjusted her position.

Ada smiled. "She is such a darling child. I dread to think we might never see her again when her mother does come for her."

Miriam remained silent, but the same concern had taken root in her mind, too. Hannah was quickly working her way into Miriam's heart and into her life. Letting go of her wasn't going to be easy.

Nick stopped his SUV near the end of the lane at the Zook farm. He knew the church members wouldn't appreciate his arrival in a modern vehicle on their day of worship. He wasn't here in an official capacity, so he wasn't wearing his uniform. It was almost noon, so he figured the service would be over and he would be in time for the meal.

Most Amish Sunday preaching lasted for three or four hours. The oratory workload was shared between the bishop and one or two ministers, none of whom had any formal training. They were, in fact, ordinary men whose names were among those suggested by the congregation for the position and then chosen by the drawing of lots. It was a lifelong assignment, one without pay or benefits of any kind.

Following the services that were held in homes or barns every other Sunday, the Amish women would feed everyone, clean up and spend much of the afternoon visiting with family and friends.

Approaching the large and rambling white house, Nick looked for Miriam among the women standing in groups outside of the bishop's home. Their conversations died down when they spotted him. It was unusual to have an outsider show up in such a fashion. Although many people knew he had Amish family members, he was still an outsider and regarded with suspicion by many.

He gave everyone a friendly wave and finally spotted Miriam sitting on a quilt beneath a tree with a half dozen other young women. Hannah lay sleeping on the blanket beside her. He caught Miriam's eye and tipped his head toward the house. He needed to pay his respects to Bishop Zook and the church elders before speaking with her. She nodded once in agreement and stayed put.

Inside the house, several walls had been removed to open the home up for the church meeting. The benches that had arrived that morning in a special wagon were now being rearranged to allow seating at makeshift tables. The bishop sat near the open door in one of the few armchairs in the room.

A small man with a long gray beard, he looked the part of a wise Amish elder. Nick knew him to be a fair and kind man. He rose to his feet when he saw Nick. Worry filled his eyes. "Sheriff, I hope you do not come among us with bad news."

More than once, Nick had been the one to tell an Amish family that their loved ones had been involved in a collision with a car or truck. He often asked the bishop to accompany him when he brought the news that the accident had been fatal.

"I don't bring bad news today, Bishop. I'm here to speak with Miriam Kauffman, and to give you greetings from my grandmother."

"Ah, that is a relief. How is Betsy? I have not seen her for many months."

"She's well and busy with lots of great-grandchildren, but not enough of them to keep her from trying to marry off the few of us who are still single."

Bishop Zook chuckled. "She always did fancy herself something of a matchmaker. I believe Miriam is outside with some of our young mothers. The case of this abandoned babe is very troubling. I cannot think any of our young women would do such a thing."

"I understand, but we have to ask."

"We have several families who would be pleased to take the child into their homes."

"Where the child is placed, if her mother doesn't return, will be up to Social Services."

"I feared as much. We would rather handle this ourselves. If the mother returns, the child will remain with her, *ja?*"

Nick didn't want a string of hopeful women showing up and claiming to be Hannah's mother. He needed to be very clear it wouldn't be that easy. "Once we have proof, by a blood test, that she is the mother, and we can see that she is in a position to take care of the child, then yes, it is likely that Social Services will agree to her keeping the child. If you do come across information about the mother, please get word to Miriam or myself."

"This is the Lord's working. We offer our prayers for this troubled woman and for her child."

"Thank you, Bishop."

Nick glanced again to where Miriam sat surrounded by young Amish mothers with their babies. Except for a slight difference in her dress, Miriam could have been one of them.

She had been one of them. It had taken a lot

to drive her away. What would it take to make her return? If she found it in her heart to forgive him for Mark's death, would she return to the life she'd left behind?

The bishop said, "You will stay and eat with us this fine day, *ja?*"

Nick pulled his troubled gaze away from Miriam. "I would be honored, Bishop Zook. I hear your wife makes a fine peanut butter pie."

"She made a dozen different pies yesterday, and chased me away with a spoon when I tried to sample one."

"I hope for your sake there will be leftovers."

There was never a lack of food at an Amish gathering. The makeshift tables were laden with home-baked bread, different kinds of cheese and cold cuts. There was *schmierkase,* a creamy, cottage cheese-like spread, sliced pickles, pickled beets, pretzels and, Nick's favorite, a special peanut butter spread sweetened with molasses or marshmallow cream. He liked the marshmallow cream version the best. There were also a variety of cookies, brownies and other baked goods as well a rich black coffee to dunk them in.

A rumble deep in his stomach reminded Nick that breakfast had been hours ago. He had already visited two other church groups that morning and looked at dozens of buggy wheels. There was no way to keep his examinations quiet. The community would be abuzz with speculation, but it couldn't be helped.

Nick thanked the Bishop for his invitation to eat and walked toward the lawn where Miriam was sitting. She caught sight of him and rose to her feet. She spoke to Katie Sutter who was sitting beside her. At Katie's nod of agreement, Miriam left Hannah sleeping on the quilt.

Before he could say good morning, she said, "I expected you hours ago. Hannah got fussy so I took her out of the house during the service and I was able to check all the buggies that are parked beside the barn. I didn't get a chance to check those parked on the hillside."

He smiled. "Good morning, Miriam. How are you this fine morning? How is Hannah? Is she keeping you up at night? I hope your mother is feeling well."

Miriam planted her hands on her hips. "Do you really want to waste time on pleasantries?"

"It's never a waste of time to be civil."

"Fine. Good morning, Nicolas. Of course Hannah is keeping me up at night. She's a baby and she wakes up wanting to be fed every three hours. My mother is on cloud nine because I came to church with her, and Bella was pouting because she couldn't come along. Now can we go find the buggy I saw leaving Mom's place?"

"That's the plan." He started walking toward the pasture gate. Several dozen buggies and wagons were parked side by side on the grassy hill. The horses, all still in harness, were tied up along the fence dozing in the morning sun or munching on the green grass at their feet.

Miriam tipped her head toward Nick and asked quietly, "How are you going to do this without attracting attention?"

He glanced around and leaned closer. "Under the cover of bright sunshine, I'm going to stroll along the hillside with you, stopping beside every buggy. If anyone happens to look our way, I hope they think we're just having a Sunday stroll."

Her scowl vanished and she tried to hide a grin. Glancing over her shoulder, she said, "News flash, Sheriff. *Everyone* is looking at us."

"I guess our cover is blown. Did you know your eyes sparkle when you smile?"

She blushed bright red, folded her arms over her chest and stared at her feet. He could have kicked himself for making such a foolish, but true statement.

He once again became all business. "If anyone asks, which they won't, I'll say it's official police business and that's all I'll say. It's my best line. I use it all the time. The Amish are so reluctant to involve themselves in outsider business that they will politely pretend they don't see anything out of the ordinary."

She nodded. "You're right. They won't ask you questions, but they will ask my mother questions."

"Ada can tell them I said it's police business."

They stopped at the first buggy on the hill. Nick did a quick check of the wheels. There were no marks similar to the one he'd seen on Miriam's lane. When he looked up, Miriam was studying the farmhouse.

She said, "If the mother is here and she sees us looking at buggies together, she may put two and two together and come forward."

"Or, she could put two and two together and redouble her efforts to keep hidden. Did anyone appear particularly interested in Hannah today?"

"Nothing more than the usually flurry of interest a new baby generates. There was a lot of disbelief when I said I found her on my doorstep."

"I imagine."

"I didn't notice any young woman deliberately avoiding me, either. If she saw the baby, she's really good at hiding her emotions."

"Aren't we all?" he said with a wry smile. He was hiding the fact that he was falling for her all over again.

Nick quickly moved from buggy to buggy without discovering the one he hoped to find. At the end of the line, he said, "It's not here. I don't know what else to do except try again on Tuesday when people go to market. The problem with that is I'm going to end up checking most of these same ones all over again. It's not like I have a way to tell them apart."

"Wait a minute." Miriam slipped her purse strap off her shoulder, reached in and withdrew a tube of lipstick. Looking around to make sure no one could see, she dabbed a spot in the lower corner of the orange triangle on the back.

From a few feet away, it didn't show, but when Nick moved closer he could see the mark because he was looking for it. "Nice. Now, if it just doesn't rain."

They made their way back along the line of buggies as Miriam unobtrusively added a dot of lipstick to each one. When they came out the pasture gate, he held out his hand. "Mind if I borrow that? I've got two other congregations to visit today."

She handed it over. He turned the tube to read the label. "Ambrosia Blush. I like that."

"It's not your color, Sheriff. It's a shade made for redheads."

He tucked the tube in his pocket. "I'll keep that in mind. Have you eaten yet?"

"No, we were waiting for the elders to finish, but I'm not hungry. Mom insists on making a breakfast fit for a farmhand."

By this time they had reached the quilt where Katie Sutter sat holding a fussy Hannah. Miriam reached for the baby. "I'll take her."

Katie handed her over. Hannah quieted instantly. Katie smiled at Nick. "Hello, Nick, it's good to see you again."

"You, as well, Katie. Where is Elam?" He looked around for her husband.

Katie had gone out into the world and returned to the Amish several years ago. She was happily married now with two small children. She understood the challenges of both worlds.

"Elam is out in the barn with Jonathan talking horses. Jonathan was just saying the other day that he hadn't seen you in weeks. He was wondering if you'd forgotten where he lived."

Nick laughed aloud. Hannah, who had quieted in Miriam's arms, started crying again. He cupped her head softly. "I'm sorry, sweet one, did I scare you?"

The baby quieted briefly, then began protesting in earnest. Miriam said, "I think she's just getting hungry. Who is Jonathan?"

Nick recounted the story. "The Christmas before last, Jonathan Dressler was found, beaten and suffering from amnesia on Eli Imhoff's farm. I investigated the case and eventually solved it, but not until after Jonathan recovered his memory."

"And fell in love with Eli's daughter Karen," Katie added. "He is *Englisch,* but he will be baptized into our faith soon and then everyone expects a wedding will follow. Quickly."

"Not quick enough for Jonathan." Nick knew his friend was counting down the days until he could marry the woman who saved his life.

Miriam had taken a bottle of formula from her purse. Nick held out his hand. "Let me take it up to the house and see if the bishop's wife can warm it up for her."

"Thanks." She held it up for him.

Her fingers brushed against his as he took the bottle. Her touch sent a jolt through his body and sucked the air from his lungs.

Miriam gaze flew to Nick's face. She saw his eyes widen. Just as quickly, his jaw hardened and he looked away. He said, "I'll be back in a couple of minutes."

When Nick was out of sight, she drew a shaky

breath. How was it possible that the chemistry still simmered between them?

The answer was simple. Because it had never died.

Katie said, "We like Nick Bradley. He is a good man. He cares about the Amish. His cousin Amber delivered both my babies. Are you going to her wedding?"

Miriam was delighted to talk about anything except Nick. "I didn't know she was getting married. When is it?"

"This coming Saturday. She is marrying Dr. White's grandson, Phillip. He is a doctor, too. When they first met, no one imagined they would end up together. He had the whole community in an uproar when he put a stop to Amber doing home deliveries."

Since the vast majority of Amish babies were born at home with the help of midwives, a doctor trying to stop home deliveries would not be a popular. "If they are getting married, they must've come to terms somehow. Is she still delivering babies at home?"

"Oh, yes. I think it took a lot of soul-searching and compromising on both their parts. Isn't it wondrous how God sends love into our lives? Not when we are expecting it, even when we think we don't want it or deserve it. He has His own time for everything if only we open our hearts to His will."

Miriam had closed her heart to love after Mark died. She had filled her life with caring for others. In spite of the good works she did, and she knew they were good works, there was still a measure of emptiness inside her. Opening her heart to love would mean forgiving herself. Was she ready to do that? She studied the baby in her arms. It would be so easy to fall in love with this child. What if she opened her heart to love Hannah and had to give her away? Wasn't it better not to love than to feel the pain of another loss?

"Elam and I are going to Amber's wedding. You could come with us."

"I don't know."

Nick came walking back with a mug in one hand. The formula bottle sat warming in it. In his other hand he carried a bundled napkin. He sat down and placed the mug carefully between them. He held the napkin out to Miriam. "Your mother put together something for you to eat."

"I can't believe she thinks I need to be fed. I'm still stuffed from breakfast."

"Are you sure? Because if you're not hungry, I am."

"Help yourself. Is Hannah's bottle warm enough?"

Laying his lunch aside, he checked the milk.

"I think it's good. Don't babies drink formula at room temperature? My sister never heated up her baby's bottle."

"I've tried, but Hannah seems to like it better if it's warm. Otherwise, she gets fussy and doesn't eat as much." Miriam positioned the baby in her arms and gave her the bottle. It was exactly what Hannah wanted. The only sounds she made were contented sucking noises.

Katie said, "I was just telling Miriam that she should come to your cousin's wedding. I know Amber would be delighted to see her there."

Miriam shook her head. "I would feel funny showing up without an invitation."

Nick took a bite of his sandwich and mumbled around his full mouth. "I've got you covered."

He leaned to the side and pulled an envelope out of his hip pocket and held it out to her.

Miriam's hands were full. "What is it?"

Grinning, he said, "Your invitation to the wedding. I asked Amber to invite you. There will be plenty of room in the church, and it's not like there's going to be any shortage of food at the dinner afterward. Half our family is Amish. Believe me, there will be food." He laid the envelope beside her and took another bite of his sandwich.

"See, now there is no reason not to come," Katie said with a bright smile.

Miriam still wasn't sure it would be a good idea. It was one thing to work with him as they tried to locate Hannah's mother. It was another thing to spend time with him at a social occasion. She opened her mouth to decline but ended up saying, "I'll think about it."

Katie got to her feet. "I see the elders have finished eating. I must go and help Elam feed the children. It was nice talking with you, Miriam. I will pray that Hannah's mother comes for her soon."

As Katie walked away, Nick said, "You know, she may not be coming back. The letter could have been a ruse. We may never learn who she is."

"I know that."

"Are you prepared to accept it?"

Miriam gazed at the baby in her arms. "I won't have any choice in the matter, will I?"

"I guess not, but you do have a choice to attend a fun-filled wedding or to stay home and mope about not having fun."

"What makes you think I would mope?"

The teasing grin left his face. His eyes grew serious. "It would mean a lot to Amber, and to me, if you come. Will you?"

"I said I'll think about it." It was the best that she could so until she figured out how she felt about spending more time with Nick.

Chapter Six

Hannah was crying at the top of her lungs. The dog was whining and pawing at Miriam and the kettle was whistling madly. With only four hours of sleep out of the past twenty-four, Miriam reached the end of her rope at ten o'clock Monday morning. As she struggled to get an irate baby into a clean sleeper for the third time in as many feedings, she shouted at the dog, "Bella, stop it! Mother, will you *please* take the kettle off the fire."

Her mother had gone to her room to read and seemed oblivious to the pandemonium in the kitchen. Miriam finally got Hannah's flailing fist through the sleeve and quickly tied the front of the outfit closed. She lifted the baby to her shoulder to calm her. Nudging Bella aside with her knee, Miriam reached for clean burp rag. She threw it over her shoulder, but before she could switch Hannah to that side she felt something warm and wet running down her back.

Miriam closed her eyes and gritted her teeth. "You did *not* just throw up on me."

From the doorway, a man's amused voice said, "Oh, yes, she did."

Great. Why did Nick have to show up when she was too tired to keep up her defenses? "Don't you knock?"

"I did. Several times."

He crossed the kitchen and pulled the kettle from the heat. The whistling died away, but Hannah was still crying at the top of her lungs, and Bella was still whining and dancing underfoot, upset that her baby was unhappy.

Nick returned to the door, held it open and said, "Bella, outside."

The dejected dog trotted out the door, and he closed it behind her. Then, he crossed the room to Miriam and lifted the baby away from her soggy shoulder. "Come here, sweet one, and tell me what's the matter."

It wasn't the first time in the past few days that Miriam felt inadequate as Hannah's caretaker, but it was the first time she'd had her shortcomings displayed to an audience.

Nick took the clean burp cloth from Miriam, tossed it over his shoulder and settled the baby with her face nuzzled into the side of his neck. She immediately stopped crying. Why she couldn't throw up on him was beyond knowing.

In the ensuing silence, Miriam dropped onto a chair and raked a hand through her hair. "Where were you eight hours ago?"

"Eight hours ago I was sleeping like a baby."

"Babies do not sleep. They fuss, they spit up, they make the dog crazy and they keep everyone else from sleeping, but they do not sleep."

Miriam didn't want to look at his face because she knew he would be smiling, amused at her expense. It was kind of funny now that she thought about it. She met his gaze and they both chuckled.

"Rough night?" he asked.

"Killer."

"Why don't you go change? I'll take care of her for a while."

"I had things under control, you know."

He smirked. "I saw that."

"What are you doing here, anyway?"

"I just wanted to check on the two of you. No sign of the mother I take it?"

Miriam stood up. The streak of warm formula down her back was quickly growing cold and sticky. "No sign of her or the father. At the moment, I'm beginning to think she was smarter than I gave her credit for."

"You don't mean that," Nick chided.

Miriam glanced at him and the little darling in a pink sleeper curled into a ball against his chest. The soft smile on his face as he looked down at the baby did funny things to Miriam's insides. There was something endearing about a man who held a baby so easily. "No, I don't mean it. I just need some sleep."

Ada walked into the room. "Nicolas, what a surprise. How nice to see you. Miriam, did the kettle boil? I didn't hear it. I'm afraid I fell asleep. A strong cup of tea will perk me up."

"Yes, mother, the kettle boiled. Nick just took it off the heat so it should be perfect for your tea. If you'll both excuse me, I'm going to go change my shirt, again. I hope this spitting up settles down when she is switched all the way over to soy formula."

Her mother said, "All babies spit up a little. You did. How your papa hollered when you spit up on his Sunday suit just as we got to the preaching. I tried so hard not to laugh at him. Is he home yet?"

Miriam exchanged a startled glance with Nick. She studied her mother closely. "Is who home yet?"

Ada's shoulders slumped. "That was silly. I know my William is gone. I must have been dreaming about the old days."

She turned and gave Nick a bright grin. "Would you like some tea?"

"Sounds great. Do you need any help?"

"*Nee,* you sit and hold our pretty baby. She's so *goot.* She barely made a peep last night. Miriam, would you like tea?"

Not a peep, but a whole lot of crying. Miriam was amazed her mother had slept through it. "No tea for me, *danki.*"

"That's right. You're a coffee drinker like your papa. Mark was the one who liked tea." She smiled sadly and turned back to the stove. "What was I going to do?"

"*Mamm,* are you okay?" Miriam stepped closer.

"I'm fine. I need another cup, that's what I was going to do." She pulled a second mug from the cabinet and placed a tea bag in it.

Miriam gave her mother one more worried look, then hurried upstairs. When she came downstairs five minutes later, Hannah was sound asleep in her crib. Bella was curled up on the rag rug beneath it. Her long tail thumped twice when she saw Miriam, but she didn't move. Ada and Nick were chatting over tea and oatmeal cookies at the kitchen table. Miriam joined them, but she couldn't stifle a yawn.

Her mother patted Miriam's hand. "Why

don't you take a nap, dear. Nicolas and I will watch the baby."

"I'm sure the sheriff has other things to do besides babysit."

"I have a few errands to run, but I'm not in any hurry. I'll stay for a while. At least until the cookies run out." He bit into the one he was holding.

Ada grinned. "Miriam made them. They are sugar-free. She can be a *goot* cook when she sets her mind to it."

"Sugar-free doesn't mean calorie free, so only two for you, *Mamm.*" Miriam reminded her.

"How many can I have?" He slipped another one from the plate on to his napkin.

"None," she teased.

"You mean none after this one." He filched a fourth cookie and added it the stack in front of him.

Miriam shook her head. "Whatever."

Nick gave Ada a sympathetic look. "She's cranky today, isn't she?"

Ada glanced at the crib. "*Nee,* she is a sweet *boppli.* I wish she could stay with us forever."

He said, "I was talking about Miriam."

Ada glanced at Miriam and leaned closer to Nick. "She gets that way when she is tired."

Straightening in her chair, Ada gave Miriam a stern look. "Go lie down. We will be fine."

Miriam knew if she didn't get some rest she was going to fall down and sleep on the floor. "All right, but get me up if she gets fussy again."

"I will," Ada promised.

Miriam wondered if she would be the topic of conversation once she was out of the room. At this point, she really didn't care. She climbed the steps, walked into her bedroom and fell down on her bed fully dressed.

The next time she pried her eyes open, her watch told her she been asleep for four hours. She ran her fingers through her tangled hair and made her way back downstairs. The kitchen was empty. Hannah wasn't in her crib.

Frowning, Miriam was about to check the rest of the house when she heard a sound coming from the front porch. She walked to the window and looked out. Nick sat in her mother's white rocker. She couldn't see if he had Hannah, but she assumed he did because Bella sat quietly beside him watching him like a hawk.

Nick was singing softly in a beautiful baritone voice that sent chills up her spine. It was the old spiritual, "Michael Row the Boat Ashore." She stood listening for several stanzas, captured by the beauty of his voice and the healing words of the song. Death was not an end, merely a river to be crossed.

Mark and her father waiting for her on a shore

she couldn't see yet, but someday she would. If only she could be sure she could gain their forgiveness.

How could she if she hadn't forgiven Nick? She pushed the screen door open and walked out onto the porch.

Nick looked over his shoulder as Miriam came out of the house. Her hair was tousled and her eyes were puffy, but she looked more rested than when he arrived. "Did you have a nice nap?"

"Better than you'll ever know. Where's my mother?" She paused to gaze lovingly at the baby.

"She went to take a nap shortly after you did."

"And she just left you with the baby all this time?"

"I didn't mind." He looked down at the baby nestled in the crook of his arm. She was so sweet and so innocent. In his line of work he often saw the seedy side of humanity. It did his soul good to realize how healing and calm holding a baby made him feel.

"I thought you had errands to run?" Miriam rubbed her hands up and down her arms as if she were cold.

It was warm on the porch. He knew it was his presence, not the temperature that made her uncomfortable. He wished it could be different. Would he ever be able to break through the barrier she had erected between them? He prayed to God that it was possible. They had been good friends once. He would settle for that again if were possible.

Miriam said, "I can take her now."

Reluctant to give Hannah up, he said, "I don't mind holding her. She's asleep. If I give her to you, she may wake up and start fussing."

Taking a seat in the other rocker on the porch, Miriam smothered another yawn. "I honestly don't know how new mothers do this."

"Beats me. I'm pretty much a wreck if I don't get eight hours."

He hesitated, then asked, "Has your mother been confused and forgetful before today, or is this something new?" Miriam had a lot on her plate at the moment. How well would she hold up under the strain?

"It's something new. I hope it's just the excitement of the past few days and not something serious."

"Don't take this the wrong way, but are you sure you're up to this?" He knew the moment the words left his mouth that he had made a mistake.

She scowled at him. "Exactly how should I

take your inference that I can't take care of my mother and a newborn?"

"What I wanted to say was you have enough to worry about with your mother's health. It's understandable that you would have difficulty managing a new baby on top of that. Never mind. I can see by the look in your eyes that you don't want sympathy and you don't want help. No need to bite my head off. I'm sorry."

To his surprise, she took a deep breath and leaned back in her rocker. "I'm the one who is sorry. My mother is right. I get cranky when I don't get enough sleep. I may not want help, but I need it. You have no idea how much I needed this break. Thanks for sticking around today."

"You're welcome. Did you know your mother is talking about wanting to keep Hannah?"

"I do."

He could tell from the tone of her voice that she harbored the same wish. Nick looked down at the sleeping child in his arms. "It is easy to become attached to her. When she isn't spitting up or crying, she is adorable."

"Did she spit up again?" Quick concern flooded Miriam's face.

Nick smiled. Miriam was no different than his sisters or any other new mother. It was all about the baby. He raised the burp rag he had on his shoulder to reveal a damp stain. "It wasn't too much."

Miriam relaxed. "I was beginning to think it was just me. I'm happy to know she's willing to share."

He smiled at the baby and stroked her hair with the back of his fingers. "She seems to be an equal opportunity spitter, but she sure knows how to wrap a guy around her little finger."

"All babies can do that. You seem to have a knack for handling her."

"I've had lots of practice with a half dozen nieces and nephews. What can I say, I like babies."

"It shows." There was a softening in her tone that pleased him. He was glad now that he had stayed.

Miriam couldn't take her gaze off of Nick's face. There was such compassion and wonder in his eyes as he gazed at the baby.

Painting him as a heartless villain had been easy when she didn't have to see him. Face-to-face with him now, she didn't see a villain, just a man in awe of the new life he held.

Did it change anything? She wasn't sure.

He said, "I meant to tell you earlier that I drew a blank for fingerprints on the basket and note. It was a long shot at best. We recovered several prints but they were too smudged to be of any use. Which is rotten luck if she doesn't come back. It will leave us almost nothing to go on."

"I believe she'll come back for Hannah. I just wish we could locate her and find out what kind of trouble she is in."

"You're a practical woman. You have to know that women who leave their babies in a safe haven are unlikely to return for them. I don't know of a single case in Ohio where custody was returned to the biological mother."

"How many of those women were Amish?"

"No one knows. The point of the Safe Haven Law is to give mothers anonymity. Frankly, while the intention is good, I think the law has one big flaw."

"Fathers?"

"Exactly. Hannah's father has the same rights as her mother does. We don't know if he knew about this decision or not. I don't like the idea that a mother can give away her child without the father's consent."

"The world is full of deadbeat dads who could care less what happens to their kids. Many of them can't be bothered to pay child support."

"There are many, many more men who would give anything to see that their children have good lives."

Nick would be one of those men, she decided. Mark would've been one if he had lived. Thinking about him made her sad but she didn't feel angry anymore. It was odd, because the anger had consumed her for so long. She felt empty without it. What would she find to replace it?

Nick said, "At least we know that Hannah will go to a loving family, even if her mother doesn't return. There are good people waiting to adopt a baby like her."

"I will be sorry to see her go."

"But you'll be able to get a decent night's sleep when she does," he said with a grin.

"There is that." She tipped her head to the side and stared at her dog. "Bella is the one who's going to be brokenhearted."

"You'll have to adopt a puppy for her."

"Ha! You do want to punish me, don't you? What makes you think a new puppy would be any less trouble than a baby? I could always adopt two and leave one on your doorstep."

"It wouldn't work."

"Why not? Don't tell me you'd take a helpless puppy back to the pound."

"No. However, among all my nieces, nephews and cousins, I wouldn't have any trouble finding a better home than my apartment."

Miriam knew that Nick was the oldest in his family. He had three younger sisters. She'd never met them, but he used to talk about them—make that complain about them—the way teenaged boys talked about their sisters. She was suddenly curious about his life. She asked, "What are the three terrors up to these days?"

Nick gave a bark of laughter that disturbed Hannah and made her whimper. He soothed her with a little bouncing, and she settled back to sleep. "I haven't heard them called that in years. They were the bane of my existence when I was growing up. Fortunately for me they didn't like the country or Amish living and refused to spend summers with Grandma Betsy. Summers were my great escape."

Miriam raised her foot to rest it on the rocker seat and wrapped her arms around her knee. She remembered waiting for him to return, eager to see him again and hear about everything he'd done in the strange *Englisch* world. "You never had much good to say about your sisters."

"True. Happily, I've learned to like them a lot better now that they have their own homes and aren't keeping me out of the only bathroom for hours on end. I never did understand why it takes a girl so long to get ready in the mornings. Multiply that by three, and you know I had like six seconds to get ready for school every day."

Miriam hesitated before asking her next question. Nick's home life had been difficult after his father's death. He had confided many things to her when they had been friends. Before she heaped all her anger and guilt on him. "How is your mother doing?"

"Better some days, worse other days. I know dad loved her, I know she loved dad, but they couldn't make it work. She wasn't cut out to be a big city cop's wife. She hated his job. After he was killed, she couldn't stand the guilt. She believed it was her punishment for leaving the Amish."

"I know you once said she was abusing prescription drugs. Is she still?"

"I don't think so, but I'm not there every day. My youngest sister lives close by. She seems to think Mom is doing okay. I know that having grandchildren has been good for her."

Miriam gazed at Hannah. "My mother would love grandchildren. That's why I'm worried she is getting too attached to Hannah. I don't want it to break her heart when the baby has to leave."

"As much as you love kids, I'm surprised you haven't married and had children."

She cocked her head at him. "Don't think it's because I haven't had offers. I just haven't found the right guy."

Hannah began fussing and squirming in his

hold. He said, "I think she's getting hungry. It's been almost three hours since she last ate."

Miriam sprang to her feet. "I'll go get her bottle ready."

She entered the house with a sense of relief. Their conversation had taken a personal turn that she wasn't quite ready for. It was one thing to have him talk about himself, it was another thing to expose her own life to his scrutiny.

Nick adjusted Hannah's position to his shoulder and patted her back gently. "Did you see how quickly she shot out of here when I started asking personal questions? Note to self—no matter how much I would like to know about Miriam's life, don't press, wait for her to volunteer that information."

At least she wasn't glaring daggers at him every chance she got. Something was different this afternoon. Her mood had softened. Perhaps having a baby in the house brought out her gentler side. Whatever was going on, he hoped it didn't change soon. He liked being able to spend time in her company without feeling like he was barely tolerated.

He glanced up as she came out of the house with a bottle in her hand. She self-consciously tucked her hair behind her ear and smiled slightly as she held out the formula.

The trouble with spending time with Miriam was that it made him wish for more. More of her time, more of her smiles, more of everything she cared to share.

"I can feed her if you want," she offered.

"That's okay, I'm already damp." He took the bottle from her hand and tried to shift the baby into a more upright position. Miriam bent down to help just as he leaned. Her face was inches from his. Close enough to kiss if he leaned forward a bit more. And he wanted to kiss her.

The timing was all wrong, the situation was all wrong, but he wanted to kiss her. It took all of his self-control to hand her the bottle, adjust the baby in his arms and lean back. He glanced at her to see if she had noticed his interest. Color bloomed in her cheeks. She gave him the bottle and took a step back.

Keep it casual. Don't blow it.

He could give himself good advice but he wasn't sure he could follow it. He cleared his throat. "I hope we have better luck finding our mystery buggy during the farmers market tomorrow."

Miriam took a seat in her chair and stared straight ahead. "I think we'll see a lot of the same ones. If I knew when the next singing was being held we could check out more of the young men's buggies."

"I know a lot of them like the open-topped buggies for courting. You saw a closed-top buggy."

"I'm sure what I saw was a standard variety, black, Ohio Amish buggy."

"It's too bad there isn't something to help us tell them apart."

"That's the point of all the Amish driving the same style. Uniformity, conformity, no one stands out above their neighbor."

"I understand that, but I can still wish for license tags."

"Well, unless the numbers had been three feet tall and could glow in the dark, I wouldn't have been able to see them, either. It was dark and the lane is a quarter mile long."

"I'm not faulting you for a lack of description. I'm frustrated by the fact that I can't do more."

"Are you sorry that we let you in on this?"

"Yes, and no. I know that Hannah is being well cared for. I just wish I could bring the power of my office into the hunt. If I considered this a straight child abandonment, my office could offer a reward for information. We could have law enforcement officers going door to door. We could make it hard for this young woman to hide. While I've alerted the local hospitals and clinics to be on the lookout for a woman with postpartum complications and no baby, all I'm really left with is checking buggy wheels. It's not high-tech police work."

"You like your job, don't you?"

"I do, but it's not for everyone." Hannah had finished her bottle. Nick sat her up to burp her. She gave a hearty belch for such a tiny baby, but all of her formula stayed down.

Miriam got up and reached for her. Nick handed her over reluctantly. He had no more reasons to hang out on Miriam's front porch.

"I'm glad we let you in on this, and I'm glad you came by today. Thank you."

"You're welcome. Why don't I pick up you and your mother tomorrow? We can cruise the market together." He waited, hopeful that this new, softer Miriam would agree.

"That sounds fine." She hesitated, as if she wanted to say more, then simply nodded goodbye and walked into the house.

Nick walked out to his vehicle. He opened the door of his SUV but hesitated before getting in. He knew it was a selfish thought, but he hoped Hannah's mother stayed out of sight a little longer.

Without Hannah to bring them together he'd have no excuse to spend time with Miriam.

Chapter Seven

A heavy morning shower didn't put a damper on the first market day of the spring. The small town of Hope Springs was bustling with wagons, buggies, produce buyers and tourists. Nick turned off Main Street onto Lake Street.

The regular weekly market had been held on Friday afternoons in a large grassy area next to the town's lumberyard. After a recent meeting of the town council, the day had been changed to Tuesday in an effort to draw in tourists from the other area markets held on the same day. The striped canopies of numerous tents were clearly visible, as were dozens of buggies lined up along the street.

Nick had been to the market numerous times. It was one way to meet and get to know the often reclusive Amish residents of his county. Today, he wouldn't be looking over homemade baked goods or cheeses. He'd be watching for anyone with a marked interest in Hannah as well as for their mystery buggy.

After he found a parking place, he got out of the vehicle and opened the door for Ada. She had been in good spirits on the ride to town, as was her daughter. Amish families looked forward eagerly to the weekly trip to town. Much of the day would be spend visiting and shopping with friends and family.

Ada said, "*Ach,* there is Faith Lapp with one of her alpacas. They are such cute animals. I must get some of her yarn to make Hannah a blanket."

Nick looked to see if her nephew Kyle was with her. He wanted speak to the boy and find out how he was adjusting to his new Amish family. Nick had had the unhappy duty of removing Kyle from his aunt's home when an overzealous and uninformed social worker insisted Faith's plain home was an unsafe environment. Fortunately, Judge Harbin, the family court judge, was familiar with the Amish and knew that Kyle would be raised with every care.

It took Nick several long moments to locate the boy. He was dressed in a wide-brimmed straw hat, dark pants and a white shirt beneath a dark vest. He was standing in a group of boys in almost identical clothing. They were laughing and patting the young black alpaca that Kyle had named Shadow. From the look on the young boy's face, Nick knew he was settling in well.

Miriam had Hannah out of her car seat and was settling her into a baby carrier that kept her snuggled against Miriam's chest. Nick said, "That's a nice little rig."

"She seems much more content when she is being held or carried upright. Amber brought it by yesterday after you left. It works wonders, and it lets me keep my hands free."

Nick surveyed the field. "Which end of the street do you want to start on?"

"First, I'd like to visit the tent where the quilts are being displayed."

Nick frowned at her. "There won't be any buggies in that area."

"I know, but I brought the quilt Hannah was wrapped in. I'm hoping someone will recognize it. I also wanted to say hello to Rebecca and Gideon Troyer. You know Rebecca's story, don't you?"

"Sure. I was one of the people bidding on her quilt last November when she was trying to raise enough money to have her eye surgery. Of course, Gideon outbid us all and ended up with a wife as well as a fine quilt. We are all thankful for God's mercy in restoring Rebecca's sight."

Ada said, "I think the bigger miracle was

Gideon's return to the Plain life after being out in the world for so many years. It was a blessing to his family and our community."

Miriam couldn't get the strap of the snuggle harness to fit comfortably. Nick said, "Here, let me help you with that."

She turned her back to him. He swept aside her hair to see where the strap was twisted. Her hair whispered across his wrist and bunched like the softest silk in his hand. He paused, captivated by the sensation.

"Can you get it?" she asked.

"Yup. Just a second." He straightened the strap and let her hair slide through his fingers. If he lived to be an old, old man, he wouldn't forget the softness of it.

"Why don't we split up? Nick, you can take mother to buy yarn, and I'll go say hello to Rebecca and Gideon. We can meet back here and start checking buggy wheels."

"I think it would be better to stick together," he said.

Miriam gave him a funny look. "What difference does that make?"

"I want to be able to watch the people watching you and Hannah." He wanted to walk by her side and pretend they were friends again.

"Okay, alpaca yarn, quilts, once through the market and then buggy wheels?"

"Sounds fine. It's too bad it rained. Your lipstick marks will have been washed off all the slow-moving-vehicle signs. We'll end up rechecking dozens of the same ones."

Miriam giggled, a light, free sound that made his heart beat faster. "It's waterproof lipstick. It should still be there."

He shook his head. "Waterproof. A man learns something new every day."

Nick kept a close watch on Miriam as she moved through the crowds. There were a number of people who stopped to admire Hannah, but no one seemed overly interested, or out of the ordinary, except for a pair of Amish teenage boys who followed them but never approached her.

Nick said to Ada, "Do you know those boys?"

She looked to where he indicated the pair looking at hand-carved pipes. "Do you mean the Beachy twins?"

"Beachy? Which family do they belong to?" Since almost all Amish were descended from a small group of immigrants, there was very little diversity in their names. There were dozens of families with the same last name in his county.

"They are Levi Beachy's younger brothers. He is the carriage maker in Hope Springs. He rented the business from Sarah Wyse's husband shortly before he passed away."

"Yes, I remember that."

Nick said to Miriam, "I believe I'll have a word with the twins. Walk on and I'll catch up with you."

As Miriam and her mother made their way down the row of tents, Nick dropped back and approached the boys from behind, taking care to keep out of their line of sight until he was standing only a step away. "You two seem awfully interested in Miriam Kauffman's baby. Care to tell me why?"

The boy spun around, their eyes going wide at the sight of the sheriff towering over them. One stammered, "W-we don't know what you mean."

"I'm asking what is your interest in that baby? Is one of you the father?"

He doubted they could look more surprised if he'd suggested that they could fly. "*Nee,* we're no one's *daed,*" they exclaimed together.

"Are you willing to take a DNA test to prove that?"

The boys looked at each other. One said, "We're not so good at taking tests. We'd rather not."

Nick folded his arms and clapped a hand over his face to hide his grin. "What are your names?"

The one on the right said, "I'm Moses, and this is my younger brother, Atlee."

Atlee elbowed him. "Younger by five minutes ain't hardly enough to mention."

Nick put a stop to what was clearly an old argument. "Why are you following Miriam?"

"Is that the baby that was left on the porch step?" Atlee asked.

"You answer my question first." Nick used his most intimidating tone.

"We were wondering what she would charge to drive us to Cincinnati," Moses said.

Atlee looked at him quickly, but then nodded. "Yeah, Cincinnati."

Nick considered their story. They looked to be about the right age to be on their *rumspringa,* the time following an Amish teenager's six-teenth birthday when they were allowed to ex-perience the forbidden outside world prior to taking their vows of faith. Many learned to drive cars, but those who couldn't afford them would hire drivers to take them into the cities. "So why not just ask her?"

Moses looked at his feet. "She's so pretty."

Puppy love—that was all Nick needed. "Sam-son Carter will quote you a fair price on a trip that far."

The boys nodded. Atlee said, "But he ain't so pretty. Is that the baby that was left on the stoop?"

"It is. What do you boys know about it?"

"Only what we heard. Is the baby okay?" Atlee asked. Moses looked as if he'd rather be anywhere else.

Nick relaxed. "She's fine as far as we can tell. If you boys hear anything about a girl people thought might be pregnant but then didn't have a baby, I'd sure like to know about it. Now, beat it."

He didn't have to say it twice. The boys dashed away without a backward glance.

After coming up empty at the quilt tent and spending another fruitless hour of searching through the buggies, they called it quits. Nick, Miriam and Ada returned to his vehicle. With Hannah secured in her car seat, Nick started the vehicle and headed toward Miriam's house.

At the edge of town his radio crackled to life. He pulled over to listen. The dispatcher was asking for a unit in the Hope Springs area to respond to a domestic disturbance call. A neighbor had called in a report that a woman was being beaten. As each of his deputies replied, Nick realized he was the only one in the vicinity. The address the dispatch gave was only a few blocks away.

He glanced at Miriam. "I have to respond to this."

"What can I do to help?"

"Just stay in the car." He shared his intentions

with his dispatcher, turned his SUV around and flipped on his lights and siren. In a matter of minutes, he was pulling up to a ramshackle house on the far edge of town.

The clapboard structure had been white once, but peeling paint and bare boards had turned it a dull gray. The yard was devoid of grass, but a tricycle and several toys leaned against the rusting chain-link fence. Several of the windows were covered with aluminum foil. Two others boasted broken shades but no curtains.

A young woman in jeans and a blood-spattered yellow T-shirt sat on the steps with a towel pressed to her face. There was no sign of her attacker. Nick handed the keys to Miriam. "If anything happens, if you feel unsafe at all, I want you to get out of here. There are deputies on the way for backup, so don't worry about me."

She grasped his arm. "I'm not leaving you here alone."

He opened the door and got out of the vehicle. Turning to her, he said, "Lock the doors and do as I say."

Miriam's first impulse was to assist the young woman. She couldn't sit by and do nothing when someone was so clearly in need of medical assistance. She took the keys from Nick. "I'm a nurse. I can help."

He shook his head. "Not until I know it's safe."

The words were no sooner out of his mouth than the screen door of the home banged open. A thin man with slicked-back hair started yelling at the woman. "Look what you've done now. You brought the cops down on us. How could you do this to me?"

The woman scrambled out of his way. Nick closed the vehicle door and approached the scene. "Stop right there, sir. I'm Sheriff Nick Bradley, and I just want to talk to you."

The man threw his hands up in disgust, spun around and reentered the house before Nick could stop him. The woman collapsed on the bottom step still weeping. Nick approached her and asked, "Are you all right?"

"Don't take him to jail. My husband is just upset because he's been out of work so long. He's been drinking today, but he almost never drinks. I'll be okay. Honest, I cut my head when I fell."

Nick didn't take his eyes off the door. "Does he have any weapons in the house? Does he have a gun?"

"We don't have anything like that. I'm sorry someone called you. I'm fine, really I am." She tried to stand, but her legs gave out and she plopped back. She tried a second time and succeeded, but she wobbled. Nick reached out to help steady her.

From along the corner of the house, Miriam saw the husband approaching with a long thick piece of wood in his hand. He was out of Nick's line of sight.

In that instant, she saw a terrifying scene beginning to unfold. The man rounded the corner of the house with the club raised over his head. Nick was in danger. Miriam pushed open the door and yelled, "Nick, watch out!"

Nick caught sight of the man an instant before it was too late. From his crouching position, he launched a sideways kick that landed square in the middle of the man's chest. His heavy boot connected with a sickening thud. The husband tumbled backward, the board dropping from his hand.

Seconds later, Nick straddled him using an arm lock to hold him down while he snapped on a pair of handcuffs.

Miriam's heart started beating again. Nick was safe. The emotions she'd kept bottled inside exploded into her mind. She pressed a hand to her mouth to keep from crying out. She cared about Nick. Deeply.

The wife started screaming hysterically for Nick to let her husband up. It was clear Nick had all he could handle. Miriam had to help. She jumped out of the car and rushed to the wife, placing herself between her and Nick. She grasped the woman's arms and held on.

"It's all right. He's going to be all right. Don't make things worse for him. Calm down."

Nick growled, "Miriam, get back in the car."

"Everyone take a deep breath. This doesn't have to end badly if everyone keeps their cool."

A movement at the window shade in the house drew Miriam's attention. The frightened faces of two small kids looked out on the scene. She forced the woman to focus on her. "You're scaring the children. You don't want that, do you?"

It was the first thing that seemed to get through to the distraught wife. "No, don't let them see this." She turned her face away from the house."

"Miriam, get back in the car, or so help me, I'll arrest you, too."

She ignored him. Concentrating on keeping the wife calm, Miriam spoke quietly to her. "The children have already seen this. They are going to need you to reassure them. You can't do that if you end up in jail for assaulting a police officer. Do you have someone you can call? Do you have a family member or a pastor who can come over and help take care of the children?"

The woman shook her head and started sobbing again. "Danny and the kids are all the family I have. Please don't arrest him."

Miriam glanced toward the car, where her mother was watching with wide worried eyes. Looking at the young mother, she asked, "What is your name?"

"Caroline. Caroline Hicks."

"Caroline, my mother is here. Is it all right if she goes inside and stays with the children for a little bit?"

Caroline nodded, but she couldn't take her eyes off her husband. Miriam motioned to her mother. When Ada reached her carrying Hannah, Miriam said, "*Mamm,* would you please go into the house and stay with the children. Caroline, what are their names?"

"Danny Jr. and Mary Beth."

Her mother nodded. "*Ja,* I will see to the *kinder.*"

"*Danki.* We won't be long."

Knowing that her mother would be able to soothe and calm the frightened children, Miriam focused her attention on Caroline. This woman wasn't much different than the confused and frightened teenagers who showed up at Mariam's door in the middle of the night.

Nick lifted Danny to his feet and led him to the steps, where he allowed him to sit and regain his breath. Danny looked up at his wife. "I'm sorry, Caroline. Please forgive me. I'll never do it again, I promise."

Caroline reached toward him. "I know you didn't mean it, Danny."

Miriam held back her opinion of men who hit women, and women who stayed with men who hit them. She knew the situation was never as black-and-white as it seemed. The best thing to do was to separate Caroline from Danny and get her to concentrate on what was best for her and for the children.

Taking her by the arm, Miriam led her down the block to a neighbor's vacant front porch. She stayed with Caroline until Nick's backup arrived. With a second and then a third officer on the scene, Miriam felt comfortable leaving Caroline in the hands of people who had been trained for exactly that type of situation. She walked toward the house and saw her mother putting Hannah's carrier in the SUV. Looking around, she asked, "Where is Nick?"

"In the house. He said we were to go home, and he would have someone bring him by to pick up the truck later."

Miriam glanced toward the house. She didn't feel right abandoning him. "All right. I'll let him know we are leaving now."

She walked up the steps and entered the shabby, rundown building. She spotted Nick sitting on the stairs and talking to Danny Jr. The boy looked to be about five years old. Both he and Nick had their hands clasped between their knees. Neither one noticed her. The little girl sat with a female deputy on the sofa.

Nick said, "This sure was a scary day, wasn't it?"

The little boy looked ready to burst into tears again. He nodded quickly.

Nick drew a deep breath and let it out slowly. "There is no way I can make it un-scary for you. Sometimes bad things happen and it's nobody's fault."

"It might be my fault," the boy whispered.

"I'm pretty sure it wasn't, but why don't you tell me why you think it might be."

It was a good response. Miriam waited to see how Nick was going to handle the child.

"I was making too much noise with my dump truck."

"I used to have a dump truck when I was a kid. Is yours yellow?"

Little Danny shook his head. "It's red."

"But the back tips up, right? So you can dump your load of blocks or dirt?"

"Yup. I was dumping rocks on the stairs."

"I've done that."

Danny slanted a questioning gaze at Nick as

if he wasn't quite sure he couldn't believe him. "You have?"

"More than once. And sand, too. My mom wasn't very happy with me when I did. Can I see your truck?"

Danny nodded and tromped upstairs. He came down in a few moments with the red plastic truck in his arms. He sat on the floor near Nick's feet and began rolling the truck back and forth, picking up the gravel scattered across the floor. Nick said, "I imagine you could carry a ton of rocks in that thing."

"Yeah. I dumped my load on the stairs, but they rolled down and Dad stepped on one with his bare feet. He got real mad about it. Mom started yelling at him to leave me alone, and then..." His voice trailed away to nothing.

"And then something bad happened, didn't it?" Nick waited patiently for the child to speak. He wasn't rushing the boy or trying to put words in his mouth.

Danny Jr. rolled his truck back and forth for a while, then he rolled it into the stair step. He looked up at Nick. "Dad pushed Mom. She fell and hit her head on the step. There was blood everywhere."

Nick laid a reassuring hand on the boy's small shoulder. "Your mother is okay, Danny. It wasn't a bad cut. Does your dad get mad often? Does he hit your mom?"

Danny Jr. shook his head. "No, so I know this is my fault. I wish he could get a job again. He was happier then."

"Has your dad hit you? Has he hit your sister?"

"No."

Nick nodded. "Danny, I'm going to tell you something that I want you to remember. It is never okay to hit someone, especially a woman or girl, or a boy like you. It doesn't fix things. It only makes things worse."

"Yeah, I kind of knew that."

"I could see you were a pretty smart kid as soon as I met you. Your dad is going to need some help. He needs help dealing with his anger. I'm going to see that he gets that help."

Miriam was impressed with Nick's compassionate handling of the situation. This was a new side to him, one she was glad she had a chance to see.

"Are you going to lock my dad up?" Danny Jr. asked.

"I'm afraid so. It's the only way we can get him the help he needs. Your mom is going to need you to be strong for her."

"She's going to jail, too?" He was close to tears once more.

"No. I don't want you to worry about that. A friend of mine who is a social worker will come and talk to your family about how to deal with being angry without hurting anyone. Now, your mom is pretty upset. She's going to be crying, but I want you to be brave for her and show her that you aren't scared. Can you do that?"

"Maybe." Uncertainty filled his voice again.

"If you don't feel brave, that's okay, too. There are lots of times when I don't feel brave."

"But you are a cop."

"Even cops get scared." Nick rose to his feet and held out his hand. Danny Jr. took it. They crossed the room to where Mary Beth was sitting holding a doll clutched to her chest. Danny Jr. offered his hand. She took it and jumped off the sofa. Nick led them outside.

Miriam held open the screen door for him. "Are you sure you don't want me to wait for you?"

He shook his head. "I'll have a lot of paperwork to do after this. It's best if you take your mother and the baby home."

"All right. I'll see you later." She started down the steps toward his SUV.

He handed the children over to their mother, who was waiting by the squad car. As Nick had predicted, she burst into tears and hugged them both tightly. Inside the squad car, her subdued husband fought back tears as he said goodbye to his family.

Nick followed Miriam to his SUV. He stood beside the door as she got in. "The next time I tell you to stay in the car, Miriam, you'd better do it."

His stern tone rankled. It wasn't as if she had been a liability. Maybe she had overstepped the bounds, but she hadn't been able to stand by and do nothing. She didn't want to respect Nick's authority or his abilities, but she couldn't deny how well he'd handled himself and the child just now. There was a maturity to him that was both calming and attractive. His compassion for the young boy touched her deeply. Nick had become the kind of man she could admire.

Alarm bells started going off in her head. There was no way she was going to fall for him again. She couldn't let that happen. It was easier to go back to being mad at him than it was to face the slew of new emotions churning in her brain. She scowled at him. "Fair enough, but the next time I see somebody about to swing a two-by-four at your head, I just might keep my mouth shut."

He pressed his lips into a thin line. "Okay, I owe you a debt of thanks for that one."

"Don't mention it," she snapped back.

Nick blew out a deep breath. "I'm sorry if I

sound edgy. You may not want to believe this, but I still care about you. I don't know how I could have lived with myself if something had happened to you because I brought you here."

He was right—she didn't want to hear that he still cared about her.

When she didn't reply, he nodded in resignation. "Okay, thanks for your help and now get out of here so I can worry about my job without worrying about you and your mother's safety."

Miriam sketched a brief salute, started his truck and drove out of town. As he did, his words kept echoing in her mind. He still cared about her. What did that mean? Did it change anything? Oddly enough, it did. A small part of her smiled in satisfaction at the thought that Nick still had feelings for her.

They hadn't driven very far when Ada spoke. "There is so much sorrow in the world. Will those children be okay?"

"It's hard to say. If the family accepts and benefits from the counseling, then yes, I think they'll be okay."

"Do you think Hannah could have come from such a home?"

"I hope not, Mother."

Chapter Eight

Miriam didn't know if she was disappointed or relieved when Nick didn't come by the following day. Although he called several times to check on Hannah, Miriam was left to sort out her feelings about Nick without having to face him. No matter how she tried, she couldn't see a clear path ahead of her.

That she was still attracted to him was becoming increasingly clear. That she told herself she didn't want to revive those feelings didn't help. It was as if her body was waking up after a long sleep. She had been moving through life, but the texture had been missing. When Nick was near, she noticed everything, from the brilliant color of the sky to the deep timbre of his voice. She was becoming aware that her life was lonely.

After having destroyed her brother and Natalie's chance at happiness, she hadn't believed she had a right to reach for that same kind of happiness. So why was she suddenly thinking about what it would be like to love and be loved in return?

Miriam's emotions stayed in a state of turmoil over the following two days, but at least Hannah was doing better. Her episodes of fussiness and spitting up had passed. She began sleeping up to four hours at a stretch and woke up alert and eager to interact with anyone who would spend time talking to her. She was well and firmly on her way to embedding herself in Miriam's heart.

When Thursday evening rolled around, Miriam wasn't surprised when Nick's SUV pulled into the yard. Tonight was the night the note said Hannah's mother would return. Miriam knew Nick wanted to be here.

She was on her knees planting rows of black-eyed Susans along the front of the porch. Her mother was watering the rows she had finished on the other side of the steps. Miriam sat back on her heels.

Nick rolled down his window. "Can I park in the barn? I don't want my presence to scare anyone away."

"Go ahead. There should be room beside the buggy."

"Thanks." He strode to the wide barn doors,

pulled them open and then drove his truck inside. After closing the door, he walked across the yard. He wasn't wearing his uniform.

Miriam's heart beat a quick pitter-patter when he smiled at her. She sternly reminded herself he was only being friendly and only here because of Hannah. She asked, "Do you think she will show?"

He stuffed his hands in the front pockets of his jeans. "Your guess is as good as mine. I've ferreted out the time and place of a local hoedown if she doesn't. It will give us a chance to ask around among the teenagers and check more buggy tires."

Hoedowns were gatherings of *rumspringa*-aged teenagers that involved loud modern music, dancing and sometimes drinking and even drug use. Amish parents often turned a blind eye to the goings-on, but their children were never far from their prayers. Until a child had a taste of the outside world, he or she could not understand what temptations they would have to give up to live orderly, devout Christian lives in their Plain community.

Ada said, "Supper is almost ready, Nicolas. I hope you like chicken with dumplings."

He patted his stomach. "It's one of my favorites, but you remembered that, didn't you?"

She grinned. "*Ja,* I remember that you and

Mark could put away a whole chicken between the two of you and leave the rest of us nothing but dumplings."

Chuckling, she went into the house. Miriam rose to her feet and pulled off her gloves. Now that the time was finally here, she didn't know if she could let Hannah go.

Nick tipped his head to the side. "Another killer night?"

She shook her head and smiled. "No, the new formula is working wonders. She actually slept for five hours last night. I'm just worried, I guess."

"Worried her mother won't come, or worried that she will?"

"Both."

"I know what you mean."

She nodded toward the door. "Come in. I'll get washed up and we can eat. It may be a long night."

During supper, Ada happily reminisced with Nick about the days when he had worked on their farm. Her mother's chatter was unusual. Most Amish meals passed in silence. Nick cast several worried glances at Miriam when her mother brought up Mark, but Miriam kept silent. For some reason, listening to talk of her brother no longer brought her the sharp pain it once had. She missed Mark dearly, but listening to her mother's and Nick's stories about Mark's life brought Miriam a measure of comfort. Mark was gone—he would never be forgotten. Not by Miriam and her mother and not by Nick.

When the meal was over and the table cleared, Ada went to bed leaving Nick and Miriam alone in the kitchen. He said, "It's a nice night, shall we sit outside for a while?"

Miriam glanced at the baby. "Sure. Hannah will make herself heard if she needs anything."

When they were both seated in the rockers on the front porch, silence descended between them. It was a comfortable silence broken only by the sounds of the night, the creaking of the windmill, insect chirpings and the distant low-ing of cattle.

Nick said, "I'm sorry if Ada talking about Mark upset you."

"She needs her good memories. It's okay."

From inside the house, Hannah began making noises. Bella came to the door and barked. Mir-iam rose from her chair and moved past Nick, but he reached out and grasped her hand. "We all need to hold on to good memories," he said quietly.

Was he talking about Mark or about his mem-ories of her? How would things have turned out between them if Mark had lived?

It was foolish to wonder such things, yet she did wonder.

His hand was warm and strong as he held her cold fingers. They quickly grew heated as a flush flooded her body. Bella barked again.

"Is there a chance we can be friends again?"

"I don't know," she answered quietly. She pulled her hand away and went inside, grateful that she had a few minutes to marshal her wild response to his touch. The simple contact of his hand had sent her reeling with a flood of memories. She remembered holding hands with him as they crossed the creek on the way to their favorite fishing hole. Once, he'd taken her in his arms to show her the way the *Englisch* teenagers slow danced together. Mark had been there, making fun of her awkward attempts to dance, laughing with them when Nick slipped and fell in the creek and his big fish got away.

They were good memories of a better time. Could she and Nick be friends again? She didn't see how. Too much stood between them, but seeing Nick every day was helping her heal—something she'd never thought would happen.

After feeding Hannah, Miriam retreated to the cot in the kitchen. She slept in snatches, waking at every creak or groan from the old house. Nick, if he slept at all, lay sprawled on the sofa in the living room. Twice Ada came into the kitchen to check on Hannah and to scan the lane but no buggy appeared. When dawn finally lit the sky, Nick came into the kitchen and began to stoke the coals in the stove. After that, he fixed a pot of coffee.

When he had it brewing he took a seat at the table. Miriam pushed her hair out of her face and joined him. "Now what?"

"We are back where we started from."

As much as Miriam wanted to help Hannah's mother, she was secretly glad the woman hadn't shown up. She didn't want to give Hannah back. If only there was a way to keep her.

"Nick tells me you are coming to my wedding tomorrow. I'm so glad." Amber had arrived for Hannah's checkup on Friday afternoon. After she had weighed, measured and examined the baby, she turned her full attention to Miriam.

"I didn't say yes. I said I'd think about it. Mother hasn't been feeling well, and I don't like to leave her alone with the baby."

"Please come. I'll stop by the Wadler Inn and ask Naomi Wadler to come and keep your mother company. She mentioned wanting to drop in for a visit. Tomorrow would be the perfect time. If someone can stay with your mother will you come?"

"I really don't have anything to wear." Miriam still felt strange about her last-minute inclusion. She didn't know Amber that well, and she didn't know Dr. Philip White at all.

"That is absolutely the lamest excuse I've ever heard. You know that I have Plain relatives. My wedding is going to be far from fancy and as long as you don't come in a bathing suit, I'm okay with what you wear."

Miriam grinned. "I was just thinking how nice I would look in my teeny-weeny bikini."

"Is it yellow with polka dots?" Amber's eyes sparkled with mirth.

"How did you guess?"

"No, you can't wear that. I don't want Phillip's eyes on anyone but me. Nick, on the other hand, will be sorely disappointed when I tell him what you had in mind."

Miriam looked down at Hannah in her crib. "I'm sure that Sheriff Bradley couldn't care less about what I wear."

Amber tipped her head to the side. "I'm not so sure about that. Have the two of you overcome your differences? I had hoped that this situation would help. I pray that you can find it in your heart to forgive Nick for his part in your brother's death. I know Nick as well as anyone can. I know he would never willingly hurt someone."

Miriam wasn't ready to discuss her feelings for Nick. "Can we talk about something else?"

"I'm sorry. I was out of line, wasn't I? Phillip tells me I get carried away in my quests to right the wrongs of the world. Please don't let my foolish mouth keep you from coming to the wedding. You have to come, if for no other reason than to meet the most wonderful man in the world. I won't take no for an answer." Amber gave Miriam one of her endearing smiles.

"If you can find someone to stay with Mother and the baby, I'll come."

Amber squealed with delight and hugged her. Later that night, Amber called to tell Miriam that Naomi was thrilled to come and visit with Ada.

The following morning, Miriam picked through the clothes in her closet with disdain. She hadn't been lying yesterday. She didn't have a thing to wear that was wedding appropriate. A stay in an Amish household didn't lend itself to fancy attire.

Although she was sure the bride wouldn't notice what she had on, Miriam was afraid Nick would notice. He had a way of looking at her that made her sure he could see all the way through her.

After choosing a simple green skirt with a white blouse, Miriam slipped on her favorite high-heeled sandals and went downstairs. Her mother was rocking the baby and humming an Amish lullaby.

"Are you sure you will be okay while I'm gone?" Miriam asked.

"I'll be fine. Naomi Wadler will be here. She and I will have a nice visit. Do not worry your head about us."

"I won't be gone long." Miriam gathered her purse and car keys from the small table by the front door. Should she leave? She didn't want to disappoint Amber.

And Nick was going to be there.

The prospect didn't fill her with alarm the way it once had. Nick was a good man, not the monster she had tried to make him out to be.

"Are you leaving, or are you going to stand there staring off into nothing?"

Her mother's comment dispelled Miriam's sober thoughts. "I'm going. My cell phone will be right here on the table. Nick's number is in it. He will be at the wedding, too. If you need anything, he will get ahold of me."

"You know that I don't like that thing."

Miriam crossed the room and dropped a kiss on her mother forehead. "I know you don't like it, and I also know that you know how to use it. I'm not worried about you, I'm worried about Hannah."

The frown left Ada's face. "She hasn't been fussy in days. We will be fine.

"Maybe I should stay home. I don't know that Amber will miss me at her own wedding."

"You told her you would come so you must go. Hurry now, or you will be late. There will be a lot of buggies on the road. Amber is very well liked among our people and many will want to celebrate with her on this blessed day."

"Okay, I'll go, if only to see what her future husband looks like."

On her way out the lane, she met Naomi in her buggy coming in. That gave her one less worry. Her mother's prediction proved true. There were almost as many buggies lining the streets and in the church parking lot as there were automobiles. Inside the white clapboard structure of the Hope Springs Fellowship Church, she signed the guest book and took the arm the usher offered her. She allowed him to escort her to the bride's side of the aisle.

The church was nearly full. Many of the guests were wearing Amish dress and children were everywhere. Soft organ music filled the air. To her dismay, the usher stopped and indicated a seat next to Nick Bradley.

She looked around quickly, but there wasn't another empty spot close at hand. Unless she wanted to make a scene by cutting Nick directly, she would have to endure the ceremony seated beside him. Would he be able to tell the way her heart beat faster when he was close?

He scooted over slightly to make more room. There was no hope of finding a seat elsewhere. She graciously thanked the usher, sat down, gave Nick a friendly smile and proceeded to ignore him. What she couldn't ignore was the rapid rush of blood to her skin. She opened her collar slightly and fanned herself.

He leaned close. "Hot?"

His breath stirred the hairs on her temple and sent her temperature up another notch.

"A little. I had to rush to get here." *Please don't let him think it's because of his nearness.*

"I was afraid you wouldn't come. You look nice, by the way. Those are cute shoes."

Cute shoes? What man noticed a woman's shoes? She gave him a sidelong glance.

"Three sisters," he said in answer to her unspoken question.

He turned to speak to the person on the other side of him. It gave Miriam the chance to gather her composure and survey her surroundings.

It was her first time attending a service at the Hope Springs Fellowship Church. The inside of the church was simple and elegant with dark, rich wood paneling and brilliantly colored stained-glass windows. Off to one side of the altar, a young woman continued playing the organ. It felt good to be back in church. She had avoided going for fear of running into Nick. Now that her fear was no longer a factor, she was free to worship as she normally did. The soothing sounds of the beautiful melody began to ease the tension from Miriam's body. It was then she noticed the sound of muffled crying.

Looking across the aisle, she saw a woman in her late sixties crying softly into a lavender lace hanky that perfectly matched her lavender suit and hat.

Overcome with curiosity, Miriam whispered to Nick, "Who is the weeping woman?"

Nick leaned forward to look around her. He sat back with a grin on his face. "That is Gina Curtis. She is something of a town character. She is very attached to Dr. Phillip. When everyone else considered her a hypochondriac, he correctly diagnosed her fibromyalgia. I think she has been in love with him ever since, but she cries at everyone's wedding so it's hard to tell."

Miriam nodded, and then sat in awkward silence. *Please, Lord, let this be a quick ceremony.*

The organ music suddenly stopped as the minister and three men entered from a door behind the pulpit. As they arranged themselves at the front, the organist began the familiar strains of the "Wedding March."

The congregation rose and turned to see a pair of bridesmaids in plum dresses carrying small bouquets of pink roses. Amber, a vision in a simple A-line satin gown with lace cap sleeves and a short veil, started down the aisle on the arm of a short stout man that Miriam assumed was her father. As she approached the front of the church, Miriam saw she had eyes for only one person in the building—the tall man waiting for her beside the minister.

Phillip looked a great deal like his grandfather, Dr. Harold White, but where Dr. Harold looked distinguished with his high cheekbones and white hair, Dr. Phillip looked downright delicious. He was movie-star gorgeous with a deep tan, sun-streaked light brown hair that curled slightly above his collar and eyes so blue they looked like sapphires.

She glanced at Nick beside her. He was a good-looking man, too, but in a rugged way that she preferred to the young doctor's suave features. When the music stopped, Miriam listened to the preacher's sermon about the way love allows us to accept the faults of others and how that same love makes us strive to mend our own faults for them.

Amber and Phillip then faced each other for the exchange of vows. When it came time for Phillip to slip the ring on Amber's finger, he fumbled and dropped it. The ring went rolling across the floor. The minister stopped its flight by stepping on it.

He picked up the golden circle and held it aloft. "My grandmother used to say that something had to go wrong in the wedding or it will go wrong in the marriage. Not that I believe in such superstitions, but let's all be glad that Amber and Phillip are off to the best start possible."

The congregation laughed. The minister gave the ring back to Phillip and this time he placed it on Amber's hand without incident. Everyone applauded when he kissed his bride.

Miriam glanced at Nick. He was smiling—not at Amber, but at Miriam. She looked away quickly, but not before her heart did a funny little flip-flop in response. If things had been different, it could have been them standing together in front of their family and friends. Was he thinking the same thing?

After the wedding service, Miriam descended the steps of the church. Around her, families and friends were gathered in small groups, catching up on the latest news and events of the week. People surrounded Amber and Phillip. Words of congratulations and well-wishes flowed around them. Every one, including Miriam, was happy for them. It was clear they were very much in love.

Rather than join a group, she turned aside and walked along the path that led behind the church to a small footbridge that spanned a brook at the edge of the church property. The source of the clear, small stream lay a short way uphill— the gurgling spring from which Hope Springs had derived its name.

When she reached the secluded bridge, she saw she wasn't the only one seeking solitude. Nick stood at the far end of the bridge staring upstream. His brow was furrowed in concentration. She started to turn away, loath to disturb him, but he spoke suddenly.

"Do you ever wonder where the water comes from? I mean, I know it comes out of the earth, but before it was trapped underground, it had to come from somewhere."

"I never thought about it."

"When I was a kid, I thought the gurgling of the water was laughter, delight at being out in the sun and the air again. It still sounds like that to me."

She leaned against the opposite railing and looked down at the water slipping over and around stones as it raced away downhill. "I think about where the water is going. It's just starting its journey. Imagine all the places and people it will pass on the way to the sea."

The silence lengthened between them. The sounds of the birds in the trees and the gurgling brook were soothing. It didn't surprise her that Nick was so introspective. He was someone who heard laughter in the sounds of a brook and truth in a little boy's worried words.

Silence was making her more aware of Nick's presence even though he stood a good six feet away and outside her line of sight. "It was a nice wedding," she said at last.

"All weddings are nice, aren't they? They mark the beginning of what everyone hopes will be a blessed union. To bad it doesn't always work out that way."

"You sound like you're speaking from personal experience."

"I've never taken that plunge. I was thinking about my folks."

"I'm sorry"

"It was what it was. Mom couldn't reconcile herself to living the life of a cop's wife. One day, after one of their ugly fights, she told him she wished he would leave and never come back. After he was killed, she couldn't deal with the guilt she carried."

"I've been told guilt is a useless emotion." Useless but so hard to put away.

"It's also a very powerful emotion."

"Yes, it is." Reuniting Hannah with her mother would be Miriam's way of making up for the tragedy she had instigated so many years ago.

More than anything, Nick wanted to know what Miriam was thinking. He had hidden his surprise when she sought him out. He didn't want to break the tenuous thread that kept her from running away again. So instead of moving closer, he stayed put, allowing her to control the situation.

His heart ached to gather her in his arms and hold her close. He'd once dreamed of asking Miriam to marry him. Seeing the love and joy in Amber's and Phillip's eyes had driven home just how much he wanted to resurrect that sweet dream. Did he dare hope that Miriam was softening toward him? Didn't her presence here prove that? He prayed God would show him the way to heal Miriam's heart. His every instinct told him that if he moved one step closer she might flee.

"The sound of the water is soothing," Nick said, quietly.

"Yes, it is."

She didn't leave, but stood listening to the

water with him. It gave him a reason to hope, a reason to believe they could repair the love they had once shared. He wanted that more than anything, because he was once more falling in love with Miriam Kauffman.

Chapter Nine

Miriam gave Hannah a kiss on the top of her head before laying the baby in her crib late Monday morning. She had slept for five hours during the night and Miriam was feeling like a new woman after that much sleep. Ada, stirring a kettle of soup on the stove, said, "You are taken with her, aren't you?"

"Who wouldn't be? She's so precious."

"*Ja,* I feel it, too. The love for a child is a powerful thing."

"I know I said I wouldn't get too attached to her, but it's already too late." Hannah was firmly embedded in her heart. Giving her up was going to hurt terribly.

Ada came and wrapped one arm around Miriam. "She has crept into my heart, too."

"I think we made a mistake trying to keep her until her mother came back. All we did was set ourselves up for a big heartache."

"Heartaches are part of life, child. God brought this baby to us for a reason. We can only pray that He shows us His will."

Miriam's cell phone rang. She stepped outside on the porch to answer it to avoid her mother's disapproving glare. It was Dr. Zook on the other end.

"Miriam, I need you to bring Hannah into the office today."

A knot of worry formed in Miriam's stomach. "Why?"

"We need to repeat some of her blood tests. I'm afraid her MSUD screen has come back positive."

"MSUD? Hannah has Maple syrup urine disease?" Miriam sank onto the porch steps. Bella came from beneath the porch and sat beside her.

Dr. Zook said, "Let me stress that this may be a false positive. We need to double-check before we assume the worst."

"How often do you have a false positive?"

He hesitated, then said, "Not often but it does happen. I'm sorry to worry you but there is treatment now for this disorder if the test is correct."

"Treatment, but no cure."

"I'm afraid not. We'll repeat the test to be doubly sure, but in the meantime, you're need to make a formula change right away. We have cans of a special powdered formula that you can start using today."

"I'll be there as soon as I can." Miriam closed her phone and stared at nothing. Her beautiful little baby might have a genetic disorder that in worst-case scenarios could lead to mental retardation and complete paralysis of her body, even death. The unfairness of it overwhelmed her.

Wasn't it enough that Hannah's mother had given her away? Why did God laid this burden on a helpless child? She wrapped her arms around Bella and burst into tears.

An hour later, she helped her mother out of the car and lifted Hannah from her car seat. As they approached the front door of the clinic, Nick's SUV spewed gravel as he turned into the parking lot and pulled up beside them.

He jumped out of his vehicle and slammed the door. His hair was still damp and he had one missed button on the front of the shirt. "Dr. Zook just called me. I could tell from his voice that this is serious, but how serious?"

"That's what we have to find out. There are variations of the disease. Some types are not as serious as others."

"Do we know what type she has?"

"They aren't sure she has it. That's why she needs further testing."

He pulled the clinic door open so that she

could go in. Wilma rose from behind the desk and came forward to meet them. "Dr. White and Dr. Zook are waiting for you in Dr. White's office. I'll show you the way."

Miriam followed her down the hallway with growing dread. She prayed as she had never prayed before.

Please let this be a false alarm, Lord.

When Wilma held open a door, Miriam froze, unable to move forward. She felt a comforting hand on her shoulder and turned to look at her mother but it was Nick who stood beside her. He said softly, "We can bear all things with God's help. He is with us always."

She nodded, drew a deep breath then walked in.

Dr. White was seated at his desk, his head of snow-white hair bent over a book laid open on his desk. Dr. Zook stood beside him. As soon as he saw Nick was with them, he said, "I'm glad you could all make it. Miriam and Ada, please have a seat. I'll get another chair for you, Nick."

He shook his head. "I'd rather stand."

Dr. White closed his book and laced his fingers together. "I'm sure hearing that Hannah may have MSUD is very disturbing news."

Nick said, "You're going have to use plain English, Doc. I don't know what your medical terms mean. I'm sure Ada doesn't, either."

"My apologies, Sheriff. MSUD, or maple syrup urine disease, is an inherited disorder. It's a rare disorder in the general population, only about one in every 185,000 births worldwide. Unfortunately, in the Amish and Old Order Mennonite communities the incidence is much higher. Almost 1 in every 380 Amish children will have some form of this disease."

"What type does Hannah have?" Nick asked.

"Let me stress that we aren't sure she does have it. However, in the most severe cases, a child's body is unable to properly process certain protein building blocks called amino acids. The three essential amino acids a child can't break down are leucine, isoleucine and valine. They are often referred to as the branched-chain amino acids or BCAA's. The condition actually gets its name from the distinctive sweet odor of affected infants' urine."

"I haven't noticed that," Miriam said quickly, hoping to prove their diagnosis was wrong.

Dr. Zook said, "Not all babies will show that symptom until they are in crisis. It used to be that babies with this condition showed poor feeding, frequent vomiting, a lack of energy and finally developmental delays before anyone knew what was wrong with them. Fortunately, in recent years all babies in the state of Ohio began being tested for this condition because if untreated, maple syrup urine disease can lead to seizures, coma, paralysis and death."

Nick looked from Dr. Zook to Dr. White. "If left untreated. That means there is treatment available, right?"

"Yes." Dr. White extended a pamphlet toward Nick and Miriam. "Treatment of MSUD involves a carefully controlled diet that strictly limits dietary protein in order to prevent the accumulation of BCAAs in the blood. The cornerstone of this diet is a special formula that does not contain any leucine, isoleucine or valine but is otherwise nutritionally complete. It contains all the necessary vitamins, minerals, calories and the other amino acids needed for normal growth."

"How soon do we start it?" Miriam asked. This shouldn't be happening. It wasn't fair, but then how often was life really fair? Without Hannah's family in the picture it would be up to Miriam to give the baby the best possible start in life.

Dr. Zook gave her a sympathetic smile. "Initially, Hannah will need the MSUD formula to be supplemented with carefully controlled amounts of the protein-based baby formula she is on now until we know for certain that the test is correct. It if is, I'm afraid Hannah is going to become a frequent flyer here. She will need frequent monitoring of her blood levels."

"Will she grow out of this?" Nick asked. He was grasping at straws. Miriam knew better.

Dr. White shook his head. "No. Lifelong therapy is essential. Typically, the MSUD diet excludes high protein foods such as meat, nuts, eggs and most dairy products."

Dr. Zook said, "Children can gradually learn to accept the responsibility for controlling their diets, however, there is no age at which diet treatment can be stopped."

Ada had remained silent until now. "What does this mean for her mother and father?"

Dr. Zook and Dr. White exchanged glances. Miriam said, "If the test is correct, it means they both carry the MSUD gene. If they have more children together, there is a strong possibility that those children will have the same disease."

A strange look came over Ada's face. "It is *Gottes wille* if their children are sick or if they are healthy. Perhaps that is why He brought the child to you, Miriam. So that your knowledge can help her."

It was the first time her mother had even come close to admitting that Miriam's education was a good thing.

Dr. White sat back in his chair. "What is really important is that we make sure we have correct test results. Let's not panic until we know for sure she has this thing. In the meantime, we don't allow Hannah to develop a BBCA crisis. High fever, vomiting or diarrhea, not eating, these can all trigger an elevated level of BBCA in her blood, and that can lead to brain damage. She is going to require close medical supervision."

Nick asked, "Should she be hospitalized now? What kind of further testing does she need?"

Dr. White rose to his feet and came around the desk. He perched on the corner and reached for Hannah. Miriam handed the baby over to him. He lifted her to his shoulder and bounced her gently. Looking a Nick, he said, "You are wondering if you made a mistake by allowing Amber and these women to talk you into keeping the baby out of child care services."

"Did I?"

"I don't believe so. There's no reason to hospitalize Hannah at this point. We can draw the additional blood we need for testing here."

Miriam saw the tension ease in Nick's shoulders. Dr. White continued, "No one has more respect for the Amish than I do, Sheriff. They welcome and lovingly accept children with any kind of disability as a gift from God. Fewer and fewer people in the general population feel the same way. If her mother doesn't return for her, I would hope that she can be adopted by an Amish couple here in this community."

Miriam stood and took the baby from Dr. White. "How can I get the formula that Hannah needs?"

Dr. Zook smiled at her. "We have some that we can give you. I will also give you the number of our formula supplier so that you can order all you need."

"Thank you."

Dr. Zook moved to open the door. "If you'll come with me, we can draw her blood. We should have the final test results back in about twenty-four to forty-eight hours. Hopefully, all this worry will be for nothing."

Nick stayed behind as the women left. Folding his arm over his chest, he spoke to Dr. White. "I wish I could compel you to reveal all you know about Hannah's mother."

"Sheriff, I wish I had something to reveal. Sadly, I don't know any more than you do."

"But you have seen this disorder in families around Hope Springs."

"I have. Too many times, as a matter of fact."

"I don't suppose you could give me a list of those families' names. I don't mind looking for a needle in haystack, but if I could have a smaller haystack to search, that would be better."

Dr. White chuckled. "I can imagine it would. I'm sorry I can't be more help. The baby is in good hands now, and that is what's important. I hear that you've been checking buggies all over the county."

"The buggy that left Hannah at Miriam's had a crack in the left rear wheel in the shape of a long Z. It's all we have to go on. I must have looked at over a hundred buggies, and I haven't been able to locate it."

"Levi Beachy is here waiting to get stitches taken out of his hand. He's the local buggy maker. It's possible he might know who owns a rig with a wheel like that. I'll tell him you'd like to speak to him."

"Thanks, Doc."

Nick left the office and saw Miriam waiting outside by the car. She looked tearful and worried. All he wanted was to hold her close and reassure her.

No, he wanted much more than that. He wanted to tell her that he loved the color of her hair. That he loved the way her eyes sparkled when she was happy. That he wanted to spend the rest of his life making her eyes sparkle.

A dozen ways to tell her how much he cared about her ran through his mind. None of them seemed like the right thing to say at the moment. Soon, he would find a way to tell her how he felt and pray that she might return his affection. Soon, but not now.

He didn't see Hannah or Ada as he left the clinic and stopped beside Miriam.

"At least it's a treatable disease," she said before he could say anything.

"That's right and she may not even have it. Where is your mother?"

"She's changing Hannah. I needed some fresh air." She pressed a hand to her mouth. Her eyes filled with unshed tears. "I'm so scared for her, Nick. Any illness she gets could result in permanent brain damage. A bad cold, the flu…"

Nick wrapped his arms around her and pulled her close. He pressed a kiss to her forehead. "I know you're scared. I'm scared, too."

Her arms crept around his shoulders. To his surprise, she returned his hug. "How is a teenage Amish mother going to handle this if I'm terrified and I'm a critical care nurse?"

"Maybe we should stop looking for her." Nick held his breath as he waited for Miriam's reply.

Softly, she said, "I've thought of that. Hannah is so easy to love. The longer she stays with me the harder it's going to be to give her up. Now that I know she may be sick, I can't bear to let her go."

Nick stepped back and held Miriam at arm's length. "There may be a way for you to keep her. Have you heard of being a treatment foster parent?"

"Of course I've heard of it. They are foster parents that provide medical care to children with emotional or serious medical problems."

"Right. There is an agency called The Children's Haven, Incorporated. They cover foster children in Ohio and Indiana. I might be wrong, but I would think a registered nurse, who's already a foster parent in Ohio, would have an easy time becoming one for them. If I were you, I'd start making phone calls."

"How do you know about this?"

"It's called the internet. Ten minutes with a search engine was all it took."

"And when did you do this search?"

"Last Monday after I left your place.

"We didn't know about Hannah's condition then."

"I've watched you with her. You looked at her the way other mothers look at their babies. I can see that you love her, even when she's throwing up on you. Since I knew you were already a foster parent, I wanted to see if there was a way for you to keep her. It seemed worth a shot to do some research."

"I'm stunned."

"The Children's Haven was one of the sites I ran across. Now that she may have this disorder, it makes me believe that God intends for you to take care of her."

Nick's revelation was a stunning one. Miriam wanted to believe she might be more than a temporary part of God's plan for Hannah. "Do you really think so, Nick?"

"He had some reason to lead Hannah's mother to your house."

The clinic door opened and a young Amish man came out. He wore dark trousers and a pale blue shirt and sported a straw hat on his head of curly brown hair. He was clean shaven. Only married Amish men wore beards. He had a thick dressing around his left hand.

He stopped in front of Nick, but wouldn't meet his eyes. It took him a moment to speak. "I'm Levi Beachy. The doctor said…ya wanted to know about a buggy with a broken rim."

Miriam and Nick exchanged a quick glance. Nick said, "Yes."

"It was my buggy. I replaced the wheel rim two days ago." His face grew beet-red as he spoke.

"Did you visit Miriam Kauffman's farm a week ago on Thursday night?"

"*Nee,* I did not." The man looked up at last. Miriam realized he was painfully shy. He took a step back and tried to hurry away, but Nick called out, "Do you have twin brothers about sixteen years old?"

He stopped, but he didn't meet Nick's gaze. "I do."

"Could they have taken your buggy without you knowing it?"

"What night did you say that was?"

"It would have been a Thursday night."

Levi rubbed the back of his neck. "My best mare came up lame on Friday morning for no reason. I mentioned it to the boys, they didn't say anything, but I did wonder if they'd taken her out and driven her hard. I don't like to pry."

Nick said, "I need to talk to those boys."

"They're at home." Levi nodded to the Sheriff and walked away down the street.

Miriam said, "I should come with you."

"I can handle it."

She said, "I know you can handle it. I also know that I am less intimidating than you are. They might be more willing to confide in me."

He considered it for a moment and said, "All right, we'll go out there together, but let's take Hannah and your mother home first."

"What shall we tell Mom?"

"The truth. That we're checking a lead, but it could be a wild-goose chase."

Miriam agreed. After taking her mother and

the baby back to the farm, Miriam climbed into Nick's SUV for the trip back.

"I had a feeling those two boys knew more than they were saying." Nick sped up to pass a wagon pulled by two large draft horses.

"When did you talk to them?"

"The day of the market, I saw them following you and I asked them what their interest was. They said they wanted to find out how much you would charge to drive them to Cincinnati. I don't think either one of them is the father. You should've seen their faces when I asked them point-blank if they were."

Miriam said, "I believe the buggy shop is on the east side of town."

"I know where it is. It used to belong to Sarah Wyse's husband before he died."

A few minutes later, they pulled into a lot with buggies ringing the perimeter. They were in all stages of construction and repair.

Miriam saw a young woman sweeping the front steps of the office. She stopped work, and waited until Nick and Miriam approached. "Good day. I'm Grace Beachy, how may I help you?"

Nick said, "You can tell us how to find Atlee and Moses."

"My brothers are chopping wood behind house. Shall I get them for you?"

Nick shook his head. "I'll find them."

Miriam remained silent and followed his lead. Behind the small house, the twins were splitting logs at such a rapid pace than Miriam knew it had to be a contest.

One of them, she couldn't tell them apart, caught sight of her and stopped swinging. A wary look crossed his face. He spoke to his brother who instantly stopped working as well.

Nick surveyed them closely. "Afternoon. Which one of you is winning?"

"I reckon we're about tied."

Nick pointed to the ground. "I want both of you to put your axes down and answer a few questions."

One rolled his eyes at his brother. "Told you that you didn't fool him, Moses."

"You should hush, Atlee." They both laid their axes aside.

Nick stepped closer and towered over the two of them. "No, I want you to keep talking. A week ago on Thursday night, a buggy with a cracked rim on the left rear wheel drove up to Ada Kauffman's place and left a baby on her doorstep. I don't think you know how much trouble you are in. You had better tell me everything I want to know."

Atlee looked at Miriam. "The baby was all right, wasn't it?"

"Where is her mother?" Nick demanded.

The two boys looked at each other. Atlee said, "I told you it was a bad idea."

"Like you wanted to bring it home and say, Levi, look what we found while we was over to Millersburg without you knowing it? We'd be chopping wood until Christmas."

Nick growled, "Anything your brother would do or say will pale in comparison to spending time in jail. Where is the mother?"

Atlee spread his hands wide. "We don't know. We sneaked out after Levi went to bed and took the buggy into Sugarcreek. We left the buggy there and went to see a movie in Millersburg with some *Englisch* friends."

"Friends?" Nick arched one eyebrow.

Atlee said, "Girls we met a few weeks ago at a hoedown. One of them has a car."

Moses said, "After the movie we came straight back to the buggy and home."

"Well, we meant to come straight home," Atlee conceded.

"We didn't know the baby was in the buggy until we were almost to the Kauffman place."

Miriam held up one hand. "Wait a minute. Someone put the baby in your buggy while you were at the movies?"

The twins nodded. Miriam tried to wrap her

brain around what they were saying. "You don't know who did it?"

"No, honest we don't," Atlee insisted.

"How did you boys know that I was a nurse?" She glanced between their faces.

They looked at each other and shook their heads. Moses said, "We didn't."

Nick stepped closer with a fierce scowl darkening his face. "I don't believe you."

Atlee's eyes widened in fear. "It's true. We left the buggy in the parking lot at the convenience store. On the way home, we stopped when we heard the baby crying. Who would give us a baby? We didn't know what to do. We couldn't take it home with us, cause then Levi would know we'd been sneaking away. Moses knew Ada Kauffman didn't have grandchildren. We thought she might like a baby, and her farm was the closest."

Nick turned away and ran a hand through his hair. "This is unbelievable."

"It's the truth." Atlee looked ready to cry.

Nick paced across the grass and came back. "Hannah's mother didn't choose a safe place for her. She stashed her in the back of a buggy in a parking lot. We're lucky she didn't pick a trash can instead. These two just dropped her at the closest farm. This is child abandonment and child endangerment with reckless disregard for the baby's safety. I've wasted more than a week of investigation time."

Miriam pressed her hands to her moth. "Oh, that poor, poor woman. She must be dying inside since no one returned with her child. How terrible it must have been to wait for someone who never came, and now she has no idea where her baby is or even if she is safe."

Chapter Ten

Nick struggled to rein in his anger and frustration. He had no one but himself to blame for the situation. He had allowed his feelings for Miriam to override his sense of duty and his better judgment.

Atlee Beachy and his brother Moses fidgeted as they waited for him to say something. He let them wait. All he had to show for a week of investigative work was a pair of scared sixteen-year-olds worried that they were going to jail or that their brother would be mad.

They had every right to worry. He did, too. They had all helped cover up a crime, but he was the one who should've known better.

"What do we do now?" Miriam asked.

He looked into her beautiful green eyes so filled with concern. Any second now, she was going to realize that Hannah had to go into protective custody. She was an abandoned child in need of care. The law was very clear on what he had to do.

He said, "We can't keep waiting for her Amish mother to reappear. Unless she reports her baby as missing, our hands are tied."

Her eyes widened and he knew the reality of the situation was sinking in. He would have to take Hannah away from her and her mother.

His heart ached for the pain he knew she was going through. The pain he was causing.

He laid a hand on her shoulder. "We don't know that Hannah's mother is even Amish. The note didn't say that. We only assumed it."

He had a crime scene that spread from one end of his county to the other. After so long, he could only pray he'd find some leads to follow.

"Are we in trouble?" Moses Beachy's voice cracked when he spoke.

"Yes!" Nick snapped as he spun back toward them. He was tempted to haul them down to the station just to make himself feel better, but it probably wouldn't help.

He said, "I am going to impound the buggy and have a forensic team go over it with a fine-tooth comb. Hopefully, there is still some evidence left. Are you sure you didn't see who left the baby?"

They shook their heads. "All we saw was a bad movie," Atlee said.

Glaring at the boys, Nick said, "I should take you both in for child endangerment. Did it even cross your minds that you should notify the authorities when you found her?"

"We did think about taking her to Bishop Zook," Atlee admitted.

Miriam laid a hand on Nick's arm. "It won't do any good to arrest them."

"It will make me feel better."

"But it won't get us any closer to finding Hannah's mother."

"The odds of us locating her now are next to nothing. Even if she came back, as she said she would, her baby wasn't there and she didn't report her as missing. Atlee, Moses, go tell your brother that someone from the sheriff's office will come to pick up the buggy. And tell him why."

They took off leaving him alone with Miriam. She said, "This is all my fault. I should've let you start an investigation right away."

"There is enough fault to go around." He headed toward his truck. She followed behind him. Opening the driver's-side door, he picked up his radio and started giving instructions to the dispatch desk. When he finished, he looked up to see Levi Beachy striding toward him with two chastened boys at his heels.

Levi stopped beside Nick. "My brothers have told me what they did. They wish to help in any way they can."

"I want them to separately write out what went on the entire time they were gone from home. One of my deputies will be out later to question them. If they think of anything else that might help, I want you to call me."

"*Ja,* it will be as you say." Levi spoke to his brothers in quick Pennsylvania Dutch. Nick didn't understand all the words but he recognized the tone. The twins were going to be chopping wood until long past Christmas.

When they left, Nick turned to Miriam. With a sinking feeling in his stomach, he said, "I need to go pick up Hannah."

"No. Isn't there something you can do? Some way she can stay with us?" Her eyes pleaded with him to agree. He was going to give her one more reason to hate him.

"I've got no choice in the matter, Miriam. I'm sorry."

Miriam could see that it would be useless to argue with Nick. She'd opened her heart to Hannah and now she was paying the price. Why had she done something so stupid when she knew how much it hurt to lose her?

Nick said, "Get in. I have to get rolling on this."

He was angry and he had every right to be upset. He loved Hannah, too. This couldn't be easy for him.

Miriam went around the SUV and climbed in. As soon as she clicked her seat belt, he sped out of the parking lot and onto the highway. He didn't slow down until he reached her mother's lane.

When he stopped in front of her house, she hesitated to get out. "Mother is going to be upset. She's become so attached to Hannah. That baby has become the grandchild she never had."

He bowed his head and closed his eyes. "I know. I don't want to do this."

"Is there a chance she could be returned to us?" Miriam was ready to grasp at straws.

He shifted in his seat to face her. "Now that we know her mother abandoned her, she won't be put up for adoption anytime soon. Efforts have to be made to locate family and see if there is anyone suitable to take her. Her placement will be up to Child Protective Services and Judge Harbin."

"I'm sorry, Nick."

He looked toward the house. "We should go in."

"I know." She didn't move.

Miriam sat beside him in silence for a few more minutes. He finally opened his door and put an end to their procrastination. Miriam followed him to the house with lagging steps.

Inside, Ada was rocking Hannah and singing a lullaby. She looked up with a happy grin. "She is such a charmer. She smiled at me. I don't believe she is sick. The doctors are wrong about that. They are wrong about things all the time."

Miriam crossed the kitchen and knelt beside her mother's chair. "*Mamm,* there is something we need to tell you."

Ada's grin faded. "What is it, Miriam? You look so serious."

Nick stepped up. "We went to see Levi Beachy, the buggy maker."

Ada held Hannah closer. "Does he know something about our baby's mother?"

Miriam nodded. "It was his buggy that left the mark on our lane. His brothers took the buggy without his knowledge."

"Boys will be boys. The twins are in their *rumspringa.* So why did they come here?"

Nick said, "They drove to Sugarcreek and met some friend who took them to see a movie. While they were there, someone left Hannah in their buggy. They don't know who it was. When they realized what had happened, they were near your lane and decided to leave Hannah with you."

Miriam laid a hand on her mother's arm. "Hannah's mother may not be Amish. She won't be coming for her. She doesn't know where she is."

"That is *goot*. Hannah can stay with us, *ja?*"

"No, *Mamm*. Hannah can't stay with us anymore. She has to go with Nick. She must go with the *Englisch*. It is the law. They will find a wonderful home for her with parents who will love and care for her."

"I can love and care for her." Ada pressed the baby against her chest so tightly that Hannah began to fuss.

Nick dropped to one knee beside the rocker. "I'm sorry, Ada. She must come with me. Please let me have her. Don't make this any harder."

"No. You can't take my boy away from me and then take this baby, too. It isn't right." She began to sob.

"It's all right, mother. It will be okay." Miriam gently took the baby from her mother's arms. She rose to her feet and carried the baby to her crib.

"Ada? Ada, what's wrong?"

Miriam turned around when she heard the panic in Nick's voice. Her mother was slumped in her chair holding her left arm across her chest. Her face was ashen colored, and twisted into a grimace of pain. Miriam hurried to her side. "*Mamm,* are you all right?"

"I can't...get my breath," Ada gasped.

Nick jerked his phone from his pocket. "I'm calling 9-1-1."

Miriam laid a hand on her mother's forehead. Her skin was cool and clammy. Grasping Ada's wrist, she felt a weak irregular pulse. It wasn't a good. She looked up at Nick. "Tell them to hurry."

Miriam felt her mother's pockets until she located a small vial of pills. Pulling it out, she shook one into her palm. "Take one of your nitroglycerin. It will help with the pain.

When her mother had done as she asked, Miriam jumped to her feet and raced into her mother's bedroom. She grabbed the oxygen canister and mask from closet and returned to the kitchen as quickly as she could. Turning on the oxygen, she placed the mask gently over her mother's face. "Try to take deep slow breaths."

Nick snapped his phone shut. "The ambulance is on its way. They should be here in twenty minutes."

This was her worst nightmare coming true. She was going to watch her mother struggling for breath and die waiting for an ambulance to reach their rural home.

Nick said, "It will be quicker if we take her and head toward them."

Without waiting for her to agree, he lifted Ada from her chair. Galvanized into action, Miriam grabbed the oxygen tank and followed behind him as he carried her mother to his SUV. Miriam opened the door to the backseat and climbed in. Nick gently laid her mother on the seat with her head pillow on Miriam's lap.

He said, "I'll get Hannah."

Miriam cupped her mother's face. "You're going to be fine, mother. We'll get you to the hospital in no time."

Ada tried to speak. Miriam had to pull the mask away from her face to hear what she was saying.

"I am in God's hands. His will be done. I love you, child."

"I love you, too."

A few minutes later, Nick raced out of the house with the baby in her carrier. As he opened the passenger's side front door, Miriam said, "She can't ride up front."

"She can in this vehicle. I can turn the passenger side airbag off. Don't worry, Miriam, I won't let anything happen to her."

He slammed the door, raced around and got

in behind the wheel. The engine roared to life as he sped out of the yard and down the lane with Bella running behind them barking madly.

Chapter Eleven

It was the longest ride of Miriam's life. Nick tore down the highway with lights and siren blazing. There was nothing she could do but hold her mother's head, keep the oxygen mask on her face, tell her that everything was going to be okay and pray that she wasn't lying.

Please, God, please let her be okay. She loves you so much, but please don't take her away from me.

They met the ambulance ten minutes after leaving the farmhouse. The paramedics were efficient, competent and sympathetic. The road-side transfer went smoothly. Miriam tried to summon her nursing expertise, but she couldn't. At the moment, she wasn't a critical care nurse, she was a terrified woman whose mother might be dying.

Once her mother was inside the ambulance,

hooked up to an IV and on a heart monitor, Miriam was able to relax a little. She could read and analyze the information the equipment provided. Not knowing what was happening was the hardest part.

It wasn't until the ambulance crew started to close the doors that she realized Nick was standing outside with Hannah in his arms.

Tears sprang to Miriam's eyes. Was this the last time she would ever see the baby? She prayed, not for herself, but for the child she loved.

Please, Lord, if it is Your will that she go away from me, hold her in Your hand no matter where she goes in her life.

She met Nick's gaze. "Can you follow us to the hospital?"

"Of course." He nodded to the driver who closed the door blocking them from her sight.

The remainder of the trip to the hospital was a blur for Miriam as she concentrated on her mother's pale face, her ragged breathing and the green blip steadily crossing the surface of the portable monitor.

In the emergency room, her training started to kick in again. She shared her mother's recent cardiac history with the attending physician and was pleased when he immediately consulted her cardiologist. Her mother was transferred to the coronary care unit after her doctor arrived at the hospital. It wasn't until Ada was taken for a heart catheterization procedure that Miriam had time to think about Nick and Hannah.

She found them in the waiting room outside the intensive care unit. Nick was feeding the baby and didn't see Miriam. Her carrier sat on the floor at his feet. He was alone in the room except for the infant he held.

His monologue of baby talk had Hannah enthralled. The baby couldn't take her eyes off him. Miriam smiled at his antics. He was so cute. Parenting seemed to come naturally to him.

He tipped Hannah's bottle to give her the last drops, then set it aside. Lifting her to his shoulder, he patted her back gently until a loud unladylike burp was heard.

"That's my girl," he cooed as he settled her in the crook of his arm and dabbed at her chin.

"I leave you alone for thirty minutes and already you've taught her to belch like a sailor." Miriam walked into the room and took a seat across from him. The minute she sat down she realized how tired she was.

"How's your mother?" Nick asked.

"She's stable for the moment, they've taken her downstairs for a heart catheterization. Her doctor suspects that one of the blood vessels in her heart has closed off. He's going to try to put a stent in to keep it open. I knew this might happen, I thought I was prepared for it, but I wasn't."

"You did everything you could."

Looking back, she realized it was true. She'd done everything she could under the circumstances. The outcome was up to God and Ada's doctors. Miriam held out her hands for Hannah. "May I?"

Nick gave the baby over. "She finished her bottle, but I haven't changed her yet."

"Leave the tough stuff for me, that's so like a guy."

"Hey, if you had shown up five minutes later, it would have all been done."

"Sure. Sure."

"That's my story, and I'm sticking to it." His teasing was just what she needed. He had a knack for reading her mood and finding a way to lighten it. She loved that about him.

The thought startled her. She gazed at him intently. He was focused on Hannah and didn't seem to notice her scrutiny. He had changed a lot from the young man she once knew. His eyes were bracketed with small crow's-feet, and laugh lines were carved into his cheeks. He smiled a lot. She loved that about him, too.

He had a small scar on his chin that was new,

or at least she didn't remember it. His eyes were the same intense blue, but there was a weariness behind them that told her life wasn't always easy for him. How could it be for a law enforcement officer?

"You'd better take this." He held out the burp cloth.

She took it, kissed Hannah's head and settled the baby in her arms with the burp cloth under her chin just in case.

If only it could be like this forever, the two of them taking care of the most beautiful baby in the world. It couldn't be, but just for a moment, she could imagine what it would be like. Much as she wanted to, she couldn't keep reality at bay. "How soon do you have to notify Child Protective Services?"

"Soon."

"Can you wait until I know that Mother is going to be okay?"

"Yes. I'm so sorry, Miriam. I didn't realize she would take it so hard."

Miriam saw the regret in his eyes and heard it in his voice. He wasn't to blame for her mother's condition. Even if the stress of the situation had triggered this episode, none of it was his fault. He didn't need to carry that guilt.

"Nick, Mother could have had another attack

at any time. I don't blame you for this, and you shouldn't blame yourself."

"I appreciate that."

There was so much she needed to tell him about Mark and about the days leading up to his death. Some of what she had to say would reflect poorly on her, but Nick needed to know the truth. Even if it changed what he thought of her.

"Nick, I need to talk to you."

"I have things I've been wanting to say to you, too."

She opened her mouth to speak just as his phone began ringing. He gave her an apologetic glance and pulled his cell phone from his pocket. "Sheriff Bradley."

As he listened, his expression hardened. "I'm already at the hospital. How soon will she be here?"

He glanced at his watch and then rose to his feet. "I'll meet you in the emergency room."

Nick snapped his phone shut and gave a deep sigh. "I'm sorry, Miriam. There are a lot of things I want to talk to you about, but they're going to have to wait."

"What's going on?"

"EMS is bringing in a suicide attempt. An eighteen-year-old girl has slashed her wrists. Apparently, her boyfriend is the one who found her. I need to interview both of them and sort out what happened."

"Eighteen. That is way too young to feel life has nothing to offer."

"Amen to that. I don't know how long I'll be."

"What about Hannah?"

"As far as I'm concerned, she's in the best possible hands."

She smiled in relief. At least she would have a chance to say goodbye. "Thank you."

"If you want, I'll make arrangements for someone to take you home in case I'm tied up later."

"I'm staying here until I know mother is doing okay."

"All right, keep me informed. You have my cell phone number, right?"

"I do. Don't worry about us."

She could tell he was reluctant to leave. Suddenly, he crossed the room and bent to kiss her. She was so astonished that for a second she didn't respond. The firm pressure of his lips on hers sent her heart soaring. Then the warmth drew her in and she kissed him back as joy spread through her, making her ache to have his arms around her.

He drew back and said, "When this mess is over and your mother is better, we need to talk."

"Yes, we do," she muttered as she came down to earth with a thud.

He nodded and headed toward the door. She accepted that conversation needed to wait until they could have some uninterrupted time together, but she hoped it wouldn't be long before she could ask him exactly what the kiss meant.

When he was gone, she gazed at Hannah's face. It was amazing how a baby changed things. With God's help, Miriam had come to understand that forgiving Nick was her first step on the journey to forgiving herself. For the first time since Mark's death, she was able to believe in the possibility. And the possibility of a future with Nick.

Nick was waiting in the emergency room when the ambulance carrying the girl who had attempted suicide arrived. As they wheeled her past him, he thought how small, pale and alone she looked. Her eyes were open, but they were empty of emotion.

One of the nurses stopped a young man from following the gurney into the exam room. She directed him to the information desk and told him someone would be with him shortly. Nick had a chance to observe the man wondering if he was the boyfriend. He looked a lot older than eighteen. Nick would've pegged his age closer to thirty. He was unkempt with dirty clothes and greasy hair.

Nick saw his deputy's cruiser pull in behind ambulance. Lance Medford got out and came inside the building. When he caught sight of Nick he stopped. "I was surprised to hear you were already here. I hope everything's okay?"

"I was out at Ada Kauffman's place when she had a heart attack."

"That's a shame. How's she doing?"

"I'm not sure yet. They're still working on her. Is that the boyfriend?" Nick nodded toward the nervous man standing in front of the reception desk.

"That's him. Said he found her in the bathroom when he got home tonight. He claims the cuts were self-inflicted."

Nick gave Lance a sharp look. "You don't believe his story?"

"I do, but I'm running the name he gave us, anyway. I suspect it's an alias. He has conveniently misplaced his ID. Our crime scene tech was pulling some fingerprints from the apartment when I left. My guess is that we'll get a hit and it won't be on Kevin Smith."

Lance pulled out his notebook and opened it. "He says she's eighteen years old. To me, she doesn't look older than sixteen. He's twenty-eight and claims he was just giving her a place to stay."

"Does he have an idea why she might have wanted to kill herself?"

"Yeah, he said she had a miscarriage a little over a week ago and she hasn't been the same since then."

Another woman who'd lost a baby. He couldn't help but think of Miriam waiting to have Hannah taken away from her. Life wasn't fair. "What about the girl's family?"

"He says she doesn't have any. She wouldn't talk to me at all. As far as I know, she hasn't said a word to anyone."

"All right, you sit with Mr. Smith until we can figure out if we need to hold him or cut him loose. I'll check with the doctor to see how soon I can talk to her."

After speaking to a nurse in the emergency room, Nick learned it would be at least two hours before he could interview the young woman. She was in serious condition and on her way to surgery to have her lacerations repaired.

He no longer had an excuse to put off making his call to Child Protective Services. With lagging steps, he went back inside the hospital to search out Miriam. He found her sitting beside her mother in the intensive care unit. Hannah was asleep in her carrier on a chair beside Miriam. When he entered the room, he met Miriam's eyes. She raised a finger to her lips, and came to the door to speak to him. By mutual and unspoken consent, they stepped outside of the room before speaking.

"How is she?" he asked.

"The procedure went well. They were able to get the stent in place and increase the blood flow to her heart. The doctor is optimistic that she will make a good recovery."

He let out a breath of relief. "That's the best news I've heard all day."

"How is your suicide attempt doing?"

"She's in surgery. I'm still waiting to talk to her."

"I hope she's okay."

He cupped her cheek and stroked it softly with his thumb. "How are you doing?"

"I'm tired. I'm sad. I'm angry."

"At me?"

"At the universe. At God. Why bring Hannah to me only to tear her away? Why make my mother suffer with a bad heart? Hasn't she suffered enough already? Life is so unfair, it makes me want to scream."

"Come here." He pulled her close in a comforting hug. For a second she resisted, then she settled against him with a weary sigh.

"Thank you. I needed a hug."

"I will always have one for you if you need it." It was the least he could do after the grief he'd brought into her life.

Miriam pulled away and folded her arms over her chest. "Have you talked to Child Protective Services?"

He pulled out his cell phone. "I was just about to make the call."

She nodded, but there were tears in her eyes. He had no choice in what he was about to do, but it didn't make him feel any better. Miriam didn't deserve this. She deserved happiness and so much more. He noticed the sting of tears at the back of his own eyes and knew he wasn't doing any better than Miriam at letting go of the child they had both grown to love. He dialed the number of Child Protective Services and swallowed back his grief when a social worker came on the line.

When he explained the circumstances of Hannah's abandonment, he was surprised to find Hannah's new case worker was sympathetic. She was familiar with the Amish and understood the reluctance of the Kauffman family to report an abandoned child. She wasn't quite so understanding of Nick's part in the affair, but as the baby had received adequate care and medical attention, she didn't intend to make an issue of it.

At her direction, Hannah was to be admitted to the hospital for observation. Once they were certain her condition was stable, she would be placed in foster care. He arranged to meet the social worker shortly and turn the baby over to her.

He closed the phone and shoved his hands in his pockets to keep from reaching for Miriam again.

"Are they coming?" she asked.

"Yes. A case worker named Helen Benson is on her way here. I know her. She's a good woman. She wants Hannah admitted to the hospital until the pediatrician here is certain her condition is stable. After that, Hannah will go to foster care."

"They'll be good to her, won't they? I've heard so many horror stories about children in foster care."

"I'll keep an eye on her and her new family, whoever they are."

"Thank you, Nick. I know this is difficult for you, too."

"The social worker will be here soon. Do you want to come with me when I turn Hannah over to them?"

Miriam opened the door to glance into the room. She whispered, "I should be here in case Mother wakes up."

From the bed, Ada said, "You can stop whispering. I'm not asleep and I hear just fine."

Nick and Miriam reentered the room. He said, "I'm sorry for disturbing you, Ada. You gave me quite a scare earlier today."

She chuckled. "Could be it was well earned, but I imagine I should be sorry for upsetting everyone."

"I'm certainly sorry for upsetting you," he said as he leaned on the bed rail.

"Old women get foolish sometimes. We think of things we should have done differently and we wish for chance to do them over. The baby is not ours to keep. *Gott* will take care of her."

"She has to come with me now," he whispered. He could barely get the words past the lump in his throat.

"Let me give her one more kiss before you take her."

Miriam lifted the baby from her carrier and placed her in Ada's arms. She spoke to the child softly in Pennsylvania Dutch and then kissed her on each cheek. "All right Nicolas, you may take her now."

He picked up the baby and glanced at Miriam. She said, "I already said my goodbyes."

After settling the baby in her carrier again, he left the room without another word.

* * *

Miriam willed herself not to cry. If she broke down it would only upset her mother.

Ada said, "I know it is a hard thing for you, but rely on God for strength and you will get through this."

"Is that how you did it when Mark died?"

"*Nee,* I railed against *Gotte* for taking my son. Grief is a human thing. No mother should have to lose her child, but we must accept *Gottes wille* for we cannot change it."

"I'm not sure I can do that. I'm not sure I can accept that the sorrowful things in life are God's will."

"Understanding his ways are not possible for us. Our faith must be as the faith of a child."

"That is easier said than done."

"Don't you think it's time you told me what is really troubling you?"

Miriam's defenses shot up. She wasn't ready for this. "I don't know what you mean."

"Yes, you do. You know exactly why you ran away from your faith and your family. Whatever fear you carry in your heart, it is not a burden you must carry alone."

Ada grimaced and shifted in her bed. Miriam moved to help adjust her pillow. "You should rest now."

Ada closed her eyes and sighed deeply. "I think you're right."

Miriam thought her mother was asleep until a few moments later, when Ada said, "I saw your brother in a dream, earlier."

"That's nice." In Miriam's dreams she searched for Mark but could never find him. She smoothed a few strands of hair away from her mother's forehead.

"He loves you, and so do I." Ada's voice trailed off. Her mother's breathing grew regular and Miriam knew she was sleeping at last.

A nurse peeked into the room and asked quietly, "How is she doing?"

Glancing at the monitor over the bed, Miriam was satisfied with the numbers it displayed. Her mother's color was definitely better and her heart rhythm was normal. The heart cath and stent placement had done wonders. "She's resting comfortably."

"Sleep is the best thing for her. Let us know if she needs anything."

Miriam nodded. "I will."

The nurse left, closing the door softly behind her. One more crisis averted.

Miriam sat down and glanced at the empty chair where Hannah had been only a short time ago. The tears she tried so hard to hold back began to slide down her cheeks.

Chapter Twelve

Helen Benson was waiting for Nick when he arrived in the hospital lobby. A petite woman with a short bob of white-blond hair, she was wearing a business suit and carrying a large briefcase. Her smile when she saw him was warm and welcoming. It eased some of his fears.

He set Hannah's carrier on the floor between them. "This is the baby I was telling you about."

She squatted in front of Hannah and said, "You are a cute one."

"Careful, she'll steal your heart before you know it." Nick stuffed his hands in his front pockets.

Helen rose. "Don't worry, Sheriff, we will take good care of her."

"Will I, or the family who has been caring for her, be able to see her here in the hospital?"

"I'm afraid not. I will keep you updated on

any changes in her condition and let you know when she is ready for discharge. Other than that, don't expect to hear from me until we've found a placement for her. How is the investigation into finding her parents going?"

"At this point, there's little to go on. Just a blue-and-white patchwork quilt and a wooden laundry basket with green trim and a note saying she would be back. Since no one has reported a missing baby in the area, I have to wonder if it was a ruse to give her more time to get away."

"Placing the baby in an Amish buggy might indicate she wanted the child raised by Amish parents."

"Or, it might have been the first handy place she saw. I've already had the buggy impounded. We'll check it for prints and trace evidence. We'll be expanding the search tomorrow and focus on the store in Sugarcreek. I'm hoping they have a surveillance camera in their parking lot. Either way, we'll do door-to-door interviews in the area. Finding the woman who discarded this baby is going to be my top priority."

Helen picked up the carrier. "I understand. And making sure the baby is happy and well cared for is going to be mine. How are your friend and her mother doing?"

"Things are looking hopeful for Mrs. Kauffman. Miriam is coping with a lot right now, losing Hannah and having her mother so ill."

"I'd like to visit with her in the next day or two. I understand she has a foster care license in our state."

"Yes, but she fosters teens in Medina."

"It wouldn't take much for us to do a home study of her new residence.

"Are you saying it is possible she could keep Hannah?"

"Finding willing and skilled foster parents to take children with medical issues is an ongoing problem for our agency. Encourage her to go ahead with her application. Who knows, it may be possible to place Hannah with her eventually. So much depends on finding the child's parents."

It was a small ray of hope, but it was better than nothing. Hannah has succeeded in bringing Miriam back into Nick's life. Her arrival had opened a door he thought was closed forever. He would always be grateful for that. "I'll relay your information to Miriam. Thank you."

"I'm sorry this didn't turn out as you had hoped."

"You and me, both. How are Danny Jr. and his sister doing?"

"The family has agreed to counseling. I'm hopeful that we won't need to intervene. Both parents realize it was an unhealthy situation, not only for them, but for the kids, too. The dad says he is willing to do whatever it takes to keep the family together, including anger management classes. I hope he follows through with it."

"I have a friend who works in construction. He's going to see about getting Mr. Hicks a part-time job. He understands the man's out on bail, but I think he'll get community service rather than jail time. It was his first offense."

"That would take a tremendous amount of strain off the family. Thank you."

Helen bid him goodbye and walked toward the admissions desk carrying Hannah. Nick watched her leave with a heavy heart. He missed the little girl already. What was life going to be like without her?

He made his way back to the emergency room and found his deputy selecting a candy bar from the vending machine just outside the doorway of the waiting room. "Any word on the girl, Lance?"

Shaking his head, Lance pulled his selection from the bin. "We're still waiting for her to come out of surgery."

"Is the boyfriend talking?" Nick looked inside the room and saw Kevin Smith pacing back and forth by the windows.

"He hasn't said much, but he sure is nervous. I'm not sure how much longer he'll stick around."

"Do you want me to question him?"

"It's your call, Boss, but I'd really like to take another crack at the guy. Besides, I figure you'll do better with the girl."

As they spoke, a woman in blue scrubs came to the doorway. "Family of Mary Smith?"

Kevin came across the room. "Friend, not family. She doesn't…she doesn't have any family."

"I'm afraid I can only give information to family members. There is a form that Mary will have to sign before I can give you any information."

She turned to leave but Nick stopped her. "How soon can I speak to her?"

The nurse said, "She's being moved to her room now. If you officers will come with me, I'll have the doctor speak to you."

Kevin objected. "Hey, how come they get information and I can't?"

"Because they are officers of the law," she said and walked away.

Lance laid a hand on Kevin's shoulder. "As soon as we find out anything, I will let you know. These hospital rules and regulations are for the birds. Have a seat, I'll be back in a jiffy."

Nick and Lance followed the nurse down the

hall and around the corner. They waited outside the recovery room doors until the doctor emerged until the doctor emerged.

Nick asked, "How is she?"

"She is stabilized but she is still in serious condition. She's already had two units of blood. We're going to give her another two. The lacerations were deep. She was serious about killing herself. We're giving her something for pain. She will recover from her injuries, but she's going to need counseling."

Nodding, Nick asked, "How soon can I interview her?"

"You can talk to her now, although she may be a bit groggy."

"Did she say why she tried to kill herself?"

"She hasn't said anything. I think we're dealing with a lot of factors, and one of them may be postpartum depression."

"The boyfriend mentioned a miscarriage." Lance frowned deeply

The surgeon shrugged. "She has certainly had a baby. If something happened to the infant, that might well have triggered the suicide attempt."

Nick held out his hand. "Thanks, Doc. I think we'd like to get a little more information from the boyfriend before we see her."

"Very well. She's not going anywhere."

Nick and Lance returned to the waiting area. Kevin Smith jumped to his feet. "How is she?"

Lance took the lead. "The doctor says she'll be okay but she's gonna be here for a while. Any idea what might've made her do this?"

"I guess it must've been the baby. She miscarried a while back."

"I'm sorry for your loss." The compassion in Lance's voice was real. Taking Kevin's arm, Lance led him to a sofa in the middle of the room.

"Yeah, well, I wasn't into being a dad, so I'm not exactly torn up about it."

Nick was pacing back and forth behind Kevin. "Dad? I thought she was just staying at your place. Now you're the father of her child. Which is it?"

Kevin craned his neck to see Nick behind him. "Um, both I guess."

"What doctor did your girlfriend see after her miscarriage?"

"Nobody, as far as I know."

Nick planted his hands on the back of the sofa on either side of Kevin neck. "Your girlfriend had a miscarriage, and you didn't take her to the hospital?"

"I was out of town for a couple of days. When I came back, she told me she'd lost the baby. She didn't seem broken up about it at the time."

"Was it a boy or girl?" Lance asked gently.

"I didn't ask. I mean what's the point?"

This guy was some piece of work. Nick hoped he could find a reason to haul him to jail since being a jerk wasn't against the law.

The man glanced between Nick and Lance. "Can I see her or what? Cause if I can't see her, then I have things to do."

The buzz of his cell phone caused Lance to pull the device from his pocket. He read the text, held it out so that Nick could read it and then tucked it back in his pocket.

He clamped a hand on the man's shoulder, "You're not going to see her just yet, Kevin Dunbar, wanted for check fraud over in Wayne County. First, we're going to take a ride downtown, and then you're going to see the inside of our lovely jail. Put your hands behind your back."

"There's been some kind of mistake."

"You'll get to tell it all to the judge."

Once Lance had him handcuffed, Nick walked out with them and waited until Lance had their prisoner secured in the backseat of the cruiser. He said, "Make sure you do a real thorough job of running a background check on this guy. Something tells me he's been doing more than writing hot checks."

"You got it, Boss. If I had my way, I'd lock

him up and throw away the key. Didn't even ask if it was a boy or a girl. What kind of father is that?"

"The worst kind. I'm going to have a talk with the girlfriend now."

Lance walked around to the driver's side of his car "The poor kid. She's too young to be involved with a loser like him."

After Lance drove away, Nick went back into the hospital and learned that Mary Smith had been taken to a room on the fourth floor. He took the elevator to the ward and asked at the nurse's station to speak to the charge nurse. After a brief conversation with her, he was relieved to learn that Ms. Smith would have a sitter with her through the night.

When he entered her room, he saw a middle-aged woman sitting in a recliner with a book open on her lap. She looked up and asked, "Would you like me to step outside, Sheriff?"

"No, it's best if you stay."

He pulled a chair up to the side of the bed where Mary lay curled up beneath the covers. Sitting down, he leaned forward with his elbows propped on his knees. "My name is Sheriff Bradley, and I'm going to have to ask you some questions."

"Where's Kevin?" She asked in a tiny, hoarse

voice. She didn't make eye contact but stared at the wall instead.

He decided it was best not to share the fact that Kevin was on his way to jail. He needed this girl cooperation. "He's fine. You'll be able to see him later. I need you to tell me what happened tonight."

She sank farther beneath the covers. "You know."

"I'm not sure that I do. Why don't you tell me?"

Glaring at him, she raised her bandaged arm.

"You cut your own wrists? Are you sure that Kevin wasn't holding the knife? It's all right. You can tell me if he hurt you. I'll see that he never hurts you again."

"Go away."

"I'm only here to help, Mary. Why don't you tell me what happened."

She gingerly tucked her arm back under the sheet. "Go away."

She picked up her call light and pushed the button. When a nurse answered, she said, "I need something for pain."

Nick could see he wasn't going to get anywhere with her, but he made one last try. "Was your baby a little boy or little girl?"

Tears filled her eyes. She rolled over and turned her back to him.

Discouraged, he left the room and stopped at the nurse's station. Speaking to the woman at the desk, he gave her his card with instructions to call him if anything changed with Mary Smith.

Dawn was breaking outside the hospital window as Miriam sat up and stretched sore muscles. A night spent in a hospital-grade recliner was a sure way to earn a stiff neck. Her mother's condition hadn't changed much through the night. She was on the mend, but her blood pressure had been all over the place.

Miriam rose and moved to the side of the bed. Ada's eyes snapped open. "It's about time you got up. It's been light for almost an hour. The horse will be wondering where her breakfast is."

"Good morning, *Mamm*. How are you feeling?"

"Better. Can I go home now?"

"I doubt your doctor will let you go home today, but it's good to see you are on the mend."

Ada moved to sit up in bed. "I'm hungry. Where is Hannah?"

The reminder brought a sharp pain to Miriam's chest. "Hannah is upstairs in the nursery."

"Oh, dear. I was hoping that part was a bad dream. She isn't coming back to us, is she?"

"I'm afraid not, *Mamm.*"

"You look tired, dear."

"I am."

There was a knock at the door and a young woman in blue scrubs looked in. "Mrs. Kauffman, are you ready for some breakfast and a bath?"

"I am. Miriam, why don't you go get something to eat while I get *redd-up.*"

The nurse's aid was setting a tray on the bedside table. She glanced at Ada. "What does *redd-up* mean?"

"To get ready or cleaned up," Ada said with a smile. She made shooing motions to Miriam. "Go get something to eat and find out how soon I can leave."

Miriam left the room and headed toward the elevators. As she passed the small waiting room beside them, she glanced in and saw Nick sprawled on one of the chairs. He was wearing the same clothes he'd had on yesterday. His cheeks bore a shadow of stubble, and his hair was sticking up on his head. She smiled as comfortable warmth filled her heart. She wanted to comb his hair and find out exactly how rough his cheeks would feel beneath her fingers.

He opened one eye. "What are you smiling at?"

"You look like I feel."

"How's that?" He sat up with a grimace.

"Like you've been pulled through a cornfield backward."

"That about sums it up. The social worker in charge of Hannah's case wants to meet with you later."

"I imagine I'll be here. She's welcome to stop in."

"She also said to go ahead and apply for a home study here. It's possible—now, I said possible, so don't hold your breath. It's possible that you could foster Hannah once you get the go-ahead from the state."

"Oh, Nick, really?" Miriam's heart surged with renewed hope. There was a chance Hannah could come back to her.

"Really, but try not to get your hopes up too much. It all still depends on finding her family. How's your mother?"

"Bossy."

"That's good to hear. How are you?"

"I'm tired and I'm hungry."

He rose to his feet. "The hungry part I can fix. Would you care to join me for breakfast?"

She did want to join him. He understood how much his news meant to her. "If you'll let me buy."

"Sorry, no can do. I invite, I pay."

"That is very old-fashioned of you."

"Yes or no? Breakfast with an old-fashioned man or go hungry?"

"I'm not likely to go hungry. I'm sure the cafeteria serves a great breakfast."

He glanced at his watch. "Not for another hour and ten minutes. However, there is a vending machine behind you."

She glanced over her shoulder and wrinkled her nose. "No, a candy bar or pretzels will not do it for me."

He shoved his hands in his pockets. "I know a place where you can get great scrambled eggs and bacon."

"All right, you win. Since I'm without a car, are you driving or are we walking?"

"I'll drive."

Miriam walked beside him as they left the hospital and climbed into his vehicle. Five minutes later, he pulled up in front of a duplex. He said, "It's not much to look at from the outside, but I promise you the food is good."

"It looks like an apartment." She frowned at the building.

"Actually, it is my apartment. But there are farm-fresh eggs in the fridge along with a new slab of bacon. I have bagels, English muffins or Texas Toast, and gourmet coffee just waiting to be brewed."

"Okay, you won me over at gourmet coffee.

Lead on, let's see if you are all talk or if you can cook."

His eyebrows shot up and he slapped a hand to his chest. "I wasn't planning to cook. I thought you would."

"Are you serious?"

"Ha! Gotcha. Of course I can cook." He grinned as he unlocked the door and pushed it open.

Miriam stepped inside what was clearly a bachelor pad. An oversize TV took up most of the wall along one side of the living room. It was flanked by bookshelves filled with an assortment of movies and novels. Opposite the TV was a well-worn brown leather sofa and a low coffee table. Beyond the living room was a small dining room with a glass-top table and two café-style chairs.

Nick gestured to the table. "Have a seat, or you can freshen up if you want. The bathroom is down that hall, first door on the left."

Miriam decided she needed to freshen up more than she needed coffee. It wasn't as good as a shower, but she was able to wash off and run a comb through her hair. Nick's bathroom, like the rest of the house, was spotless. Was he that good a housekeeper, or did he have someone come in?

By the time she returned to the dining room,

the smell of frying bacon filled the air. Her stomach rumbled, and she pressed her hand to her midsection to quiet it.

"It smells good," she said, feeling odd to be in his home. It was nothing like she had imagined. She wasn't sure what she thought it would be like, but not once had she pictured Nick cracking eggs in a bowl.

"How do you like your eggs?" he asked without looking up.

"Over hard, break the yolks. It's the only way my mother ever fixes them."

He chuckled. "I do remember that, now. I asked her for a sunny-side up egg the first morning I came to stay with you. She looked at me like I had asked for rat poison."

"I remember. We call them dippy-eggs."

She remembered a lot about that summer, and there were things she needed to Nick to understand, but not now. For a little while, she wanted to enjoy his company and pretend her secret didn't exist.

Smiling too brightly, she asked, "Where is the coffee you promised me?"

He pointed over his shoulder with the spatula. "On the counter behind me."

She entered the small kitchen and brushed past him. "And the cups?"

"If you can't find a cup in a kitchen this size, you're not much of a detective."

"Ha! Ha! You've been wanting to say that for days, haven't you?"

She could feel his shoulders shaking with suppressed laughter behind her. *"Ja, Fräulein."*

"Your Amish accent is terrible." She got a cup and elbowed him in the ribs in the process.

He ignored her puny attempt to rile him. "You've managed to get rid of yours. Most of it, anyway."

"It took some work."

"Diction classes?"

"Yes. I didn't want to sound like a hick from the sticks when I applied for jobs. I encourage all the kids who stay with me to take the classes."

She filled a cup and returned to the table. She knew her cheeks were flushed. Would he think it was caused by the hot coffee, or did he realize it was because of his proximity? When they had been close years ago she had fantasized about what it would be like to be married to him, to wake up with him, to have breakfast, just the two of them, in his *Englisch* house. Her girlhood daydreams didn't do justice to the reality of sharing a meal with him. How could she know that the intimate setting of his kitchen would be every bit as alluring as dinner in a fine restaurant? She took a quick sip of her coffee and scalded her tongue.

"Is that how you think of the Amish? Hicks from the sticks?" He brought a plate of crispy bacon to the table and set it in front of her.

She blew on her cup. "It's not my opinion that counts. I know Amish kids are naive, unused to worldly things and curious, but they aren't stupid. They simply can't make informed decisions because they lack knowledge, not intelligence. People have learned to take advantage of that. By sounding less Amish, they have a better chance at fair treatment."

He returned to the table with his plate and her eggs on his spatula. He slid them on to her plate and sat down. He bowed his head and silently prayed. Miriam waited until he was finished to ask for the salt. Smiling, he pushed it toward her.

It was a simple meal, but it had an intimate feel to it. It was a feeling she wanted to cultivate and enjoy more often. The thought had barely crossed her mind when his phone rang.

He looked at the number and shook his head. "I knew it."

"Work?" she asked. Was this cozy interlude destined to end early?

"It's my deputy. He's investigating our suicide

attempt. I have to take this." He rose from the table and walked into the other room.

"This had better be important, Rob," Nick growled into the phone. His morning had been going so well.

"Hi, boss. The crime scene people are wrapping up."

"You called to tell me that?" Nick frowned. Rob Craiger was one of his most experienced deputies. He normally let his written reports do the talking.

"No, I just finished interviewing the woman who lives in the trailer next door. She didn't get home from work until thirty minutes ago."

"Did she give us anything useful?"

"She didn't have anything good to say about the boyfriend, but here is the odd thing. She swears that she heard a baby crying over here two weeks ago on Thursday. She remembers the night because someone stole a laundry basket off her back porch and a quilt off her clothesline that same night. There's no sign of a baby inside the Smith's trailer. No diapers, no baby bottles, no crib."

All the pieces came together with a snap in Nick's mind. Mary's baby hadn't died. She'd left it in a buggy two blocks away at the Shop and Save Grocery Mart.

He asked, "Was the quilt blue patchwork and the laundry basket wooden with green trim?"

He could hear Rob thumbing through the pages of his notebook until he found the one he wanted. He said in surprise. "Yeah. How did you know that?"

"Never mind. Come back to the station. I'll be over at the courthouse as soon as it opens."

"Why?"

"To get a court order for DNA testing. I think I know where the baby is."

Nick looked over his shoulder at Miriam buttering a piece of toast. There was no way he wanted to tell her that Hannah was once again out of her reach. Still, if things were to go as he hoped, she had to see how difficult his job could be.

When he walked back to the table, she looked up and her smile faded. "Nick, what's the matter?"

"We think we've found Hannah's parents."

"Oh." Her shoulders slumped.

"Her mother is the girl who tried to commit suicide and the man we think is the father is in jail for writing hot checks."

"Will Hannah be returned to someone like that?"

"They aren't the best parents, but I've seen the courts give children back to worse."

"What do we do?"

"Wait until we have DNA evidence to prove who they are. If the mother is up to a visit, I'd like to try and interview her again. She wouldn't talk to me last time. You've had a lot of experience with girls this age. Would you like to give it a try?"

"Sure. Have you got time to finish your breakfast? Your eggs are getting cold."

He sat down but had taken only two bites before Miriam's cell phone began ringing. She flipped it open but didn't immediately answer.

"Who is it?" he asked.

She looked at him with a new fear in her eyes. "It's the Hope Springs medical clinic."

Chapter Thirteen

Miriam answered the phone. Dr. White's craggy voice boomed in her ear. "I won't keep you in suspense. Hannah's tests have come back negative."

"Negative?" Miriam could barely breathe the word as relief flooded her.

"All negative. She shows no signs of maple syrup urine disease. It was a simple lab error. It seems her report was mixed up with another baby with the same last name."

Miriam turned to Nick. "Hannah is fine. Her tests came back okay. She isn't sick."

Nick closed his eyes. "Thank you, God."

Miriam smiled through tears of joy. "You have no idea how much we needed some good news this morning, Dr. White. Thank you."

"My pleasure." He hung up before she could tell him that Hannah was no longer in her care.

Knowing that social services would take care of those details, Miriam put her cell phone back in her purse. "If you're finished, we should get back to the hospital. Let me wash these dishes and we can go."

"What are the odds that I'll get a second date if I make you wash dishes?"

"Slim, since I wouldn't call this a first date," she teased.

Some of the tension returned to his shoulders. "What would you call it?"

"I'd call it an interrupted meal."

He shrugged. "That is the lot of a county sheriff. I've had more interrupted meals than I can count."

"What you need to do is learn how to take your food with you." She took two pieces of bacon and rolled them in a piece of bread.

She handed the concoction to Nick, took his keys from where he'd set them on the counter and headed for the door. "I'll drive while you finish eating."

"Yes, boss." He gave her a quick salute.

Once he was in the truck, he ate and lapsed into silence. She glanced at him several times on the way to the hospital, but he simply stared out the window. He was deeply concerned by the thought of Hannah having such troubled parents.

She said, "Thanks for breakfast."

"Egg peppered with good and bad news. It could have been better."

"I'm a big girl, Nick. I understand that sometimes the job has to come first. It's the same in my profession."

He smiled a real smile. "I appreciate that. Let's check on how your mother is doing."

When they got back to her mother's room, they found her mother's doctor making his rounds. Miriam was glad she hadn't missed him. At least one good thing had come out of her rapid exit from Nick's place.

The doctor spent a few minutes going over Ada's X-rays and lab reports. Although he was generally pleased with her progress, he felt it was necessary to keep her a few more days. Ada disagreed, but he had an ally in Miriam.

She was concerned about her mother's poor blood pressure control. She didn't want her mother going home only to have to turn around and come back again. Or worse.

When the doctor left the room, Ada said, "I don't know why you had to agree with him. This is costing too much money."

Miriam knew her mother's church would help cover the costs of her medical care. "Don't worry about that. Concentrate on getting better."

"I'm better enough," Ada grumped, but she couldn't hold back a yawn.

Nick pushed the bed control to lower it. "A little nap will do wonders for you. Miriam and I have some errands to run, but we'll be back soon."

Once the bed was down, Ada pulled the covers up to her chin. "Seeing Hannah would do wonders for me."

Miriam tucked the covers around her mother's shoulders. "I know. It would do wonders for us, too."

Ada said, "I miss her. I pray the Lord finds a loving home for her."

"So do I," Miriam replied with a deep ache in her heart as she met Nick's gaze. She didn't know how she would bear it if it turned out otherwise.

Nick had no trouble getting the court order he needed. Since both Hannah and Mary Smith already had blood in the hospital laboratory, the process of obtaining a DNA match was simplified to some degree, but it would still take at least forty-eight hours before he would know if they were mother and child.

Kevin Dunbar refused to allow a DNA swab, claiming he wasn't the father and he didn't want to be forced to pay child support for a kid who wasn't his. By noon, he made bail. As he jogged down the steps on his way out of the building, Nick stood with Miriam at the door to his offices. "I doubt he will stay in town long enough to visit Mary. He has the look of a man who is going to skip out on his bail."

"How can you tell?"

Nick gave her a wry grin. "I've seen enough small-time crooks to know how they behave."

He needed to concentrate on this case, but all he could think about was how natural it had seemed to fix breakfast for Miriam and how good it had been to see her smiling at him from across his table.

He wanted to see her again. Not just at his table, but in every aspect of his life. He'd fallen head over heels in love with her and he still had no idea how she felt about him.

"Excuse me, Sheriff."

Nick looked over his shoulder to see his secretary standing in the doorway. "Do you need something?"

"Just to deliver this file from Child Protective Services."

"Thanks. I'll take it." He held out his hand.

She left the file with him. He walked into his office with Miriam and closed his door. He sat in his chair and stared at the folder in his hand.

"You're going to have to call Ms. Benson and

tell her what you suspect," Miriam reminded him gently.

He smiled at her. Perhaps she would be able to get through to Mary Smith and get the young woman to open up about what had happened to her baby and why she'd tried to kill herself.

"If Hannah isn't Mary's child, then I have another missing infant somewhere in Sugarcreek."

The thought made his blood run cold. After nearly two weeks, he wouldn't be looking for a live child.

If Mary would just admit she'd left the baby in the Beachy's buggy it would save him a lot of time and effort. He picked up the phone to call her doctor. He needed to know when he could interview the girl again.

When he had her psychiatrist on the line, he asked, "Has Mary Smith started talking to anyone?"

"No. I have her on a strong antidepressant medication, but it takes a while for it to build up in the body. It may be several days before we see improvement. All she has done is to ask for pain meds. Other than that, she hasn't said anything."

"I have some information you may find useful. We have a baby that was found abandoned around the same time that Kevin Dunbar says Mary's baby was stillborn. A neighbor reports hearing a baby crying at the Smith address a few hours before the abandoned infant was found. It's possible Mary got rid of her baby by placing it in an Amish buggy at a nearby parking lot."

"I see. That is disturbing news. This may be a case of postpartum psychosis rather than depression. Mary may not even realize what happened to her child. Thank you for the information."

"I'd like to question her again and mention what I just told you. I'd like to see what kind of response I get."

"I don't think that's a good idea at this point, Sheriff. I have to be careful. She is very fragile. I don't want her to regress into a more serious state of mind."

"This is a police investigation into a missing child, Doctor. I hope you understand the seriousness of it."

"I do, but I have to keep the best interest of my clients in mind when making these kind of decisions. Until I think she is strong enough, I won't allow you to question her."

"I can get a court order to interview her."

"Fine. When you have one in hand, I'll comply with it. Until then, good day, Sheriff."

The line went dead in Nick's hand. He hung up in frustration.

"Well?" Miriam asked.

"He says I can't see her."

"Can you get a court order to do so?"

"I doubt it. I don't believe any of the local judges would go against the recommendation of a patient's doctor."

"So what now?"

"We're back to waiting." It was something he didn't do well.

Miriam convinced Nick to run her home so that she could collect a few of her mother's things and get her own car. She knew he was frustrated and impatient with waiting.

Bella was delighted to see them and practically knocked her down with affection. There was still food in Bella's dish and water in her bowl, so Miriam knew the dog hadn't suffered anything but loneliness while they'd been gone. Nick took care of the outside chores while Miriam took a shower and changed into fresh clothes.

When she came downstairs, she found Nick staring into Hannah's empty cradle. There was so much sadness in his eyes that she went into his arms without thinking. She whispered, "I miss her, too."

He sniffed and wiped at his eyes. "I should put this back in the attic."

"Not yet. Leave it down here a little longer."

"All right. What's next?"

"I'm not sure how long mother will be in the hospital. I want to let Bishop Zook know so that he can arrange for people to come and take care of the animals."

"I could take Bella back to my place," he offered.

"That would be great."

Bella jumped into Nick's backseat, happy to be going for a ride. Miriam waved goodbye as Nick headed back to work. The moment he was out of sight she began to miss him. When had he become the person she depended on? Perhaps he had always been that person, she just couldn't see it until now. Within a few minutes she was pulling into the Zook farm.

The bishop was working on his corn planter, hammering a bent blade back into shape. He looked up, wiped the sweat from his brow with the back of his sleeve and came to speak to her.

"Good day, Miriam Kauffman, what brings you here on this fine afternoon?"

"I came to let you know that my mother is in the hospital in Millersburg. She had another heart attack."

"We shall pray for her recovery and ask for God's mercy."

"Thank you, Bishop Zook."

"Do not be concerned about the farm," the

bishop added. "It will be taken care of until you and your mother return."

Miriam smiled with gratitude. An Amish person never had to worry about what would happen if they were unable to continue their farm work or provide for their family. The entire community would pitch in at a moment's notice to see that everything was taken care of.

No one went hungry. No one was left alone. The Amish took care of each other. When her mother came home, there would be fresh chopped firewood, kindling in the stove and a table full of things to eat.

As she headed back toward the hospital, Miriam couldn't help thinking about Nick. Before their relationship went any further, she needed to tell him about the day Mark died. There might not be a relationship after her confession.

Nick had shouldered the blame alone for years when she could have eased his guilt by admitting her part. Would he forgive her when he learned the part she had played? She prayed that he would. She no longer blamed him for the accident that took her brother's life. Nick needed to hear her say that. She needed to tell him.

Back at the hospital, Miriam found her mother was once again having chest pain with a spike in her blood pressure. This time it was so high that Miriam feared she would have a stroke. When the staff was finally able to bring it under control, Miriam took a seat near the window.

"Miriam?" Her mother raised a hand as if seeking her.

"I'm here." Miriam moved her chair to the bedside and took her mother's hand between her own.

"We should go visit your brother."

Gently, Miriam said, "Mark is gone. We can't visit him."

"I meant visit his grave. I want to plant new flowers there. You can do that for me, can't you?" Ada drifted back to sleep saving Miriam from having to answer. She hadn't been back to Mark's grave since his funeral.

Ada slept through most of the day. Miriam catnapped in the chair, watched some senseless afternoon talk show on TV and waited for Nick to call. When he finally did, she couldn't stop the happy leap of her heart. "Hi, there. I was beginning to think you didn't want to talk to me."

"I'm sorry. I've been busy. Hopefully, things will be wrapped up soon and I can get back to the hospital. Maybe we could try for dinner together?"

"I'd like that," she answered, amazed at just how much she wanted to spend time alone with him.

"How's your mother?"

"She had a bad spell right after I got back. She was talking about going to see Mark's grave. It has me worried."

"She's always been such a strong woman. I'm sure she'll be fine." His assurance rang hollow. He was worried, too.

"How's Bella?"

"She's hiding out under my desk after stealing my secretary's lunch."

"My poor baby. This has been rough on her."

"You couldn't tell it by looking at her. She's eyeing my cheese-covered pretzel as we speak."

Miriam chuckled. "Call me later. There are things I need to say to you."

"Can't you tell me now?"

"No, not on the phone. When I see you in person."

"Now you have me worried."

"Don't be. I have a feeling that you may already know what I have to say."

Throughout the day, Miriam divided her time between caring for her mother and waiting to spend a few stolen minutes with Nick. His promise of dinner turned into a late-night burrito that he carried into her mother's room in a greasy, brown paper bag long after visiting hours. It was the best burrito Miriam had ever eaten. Unfortunately, he couldn't stay.

The next evening she had a short, to the point meeting with Hannah's social worker. Mostly, the woman wanted to know about Hannah's schedule, her feeding issues and any type of history Miriam could provide. It wasn't much, but it felt good to be doing something that might help Hannah.

The woman was leaving when Nick showed up. They spoke briefly, but the woman again said she couldn't share any information about Hannah.

Miriam turned to Nick after she was gone. "Come on. I need a lookout."

He followed her into the hall. "What are we doing?"

"We are taking matters into our own hands. I want to know how Hannah is doing."

Miriam entered the elevator and pushed the button for the maternity floor. They walked down the halls listening to the sound of infants crying. None of them were Hannah. Miriam was sure she'd recognize her cry. She stopped beside the viewing window that looked into the special care section of the nursery and tried to get a glimpse of Hannah.

There was only one baby in the nursery. It had to be Hannah. Nick would have been notified if she had been dismissed.

Miriam tapped on the window and then noticed a sign that said to go to the door and not to knock on the window. The young nurse inside looked over and smiled. She gestured toward the door.

Miriam looked at Nick. "Keep an eye out for anyone who might know me."

"Is this illegal?"

"Can I take the Fifth on that?"

"No." He scowled at her.

"Then it isn't illegal." She waited as the nurse opened the door.

The young nurse asked, "Are you a relative?"

Miriam smiled. "No, I'm a critical care nurse and I'd love to tour your unit. I've often thought about working in pediatrics."

It was the truth. She had considered changing fields more than once.

"Actually, there is an opening on the night shift, but it's only part-time. This really is a great place to work. You should consider taking the job. Our charge nurse has stepped out, but she'll be back in about ten minutes. She knows more about what goes on here. I've only worked here a few months."

Miriam smiled at Nick and walked inside. "You don't have a very high census. I only see one baby, is that right?"

"Normally we run between three and five

occupied beds, but right now all we have is a baby that is a police hold."

"I thought only sick babies were admitted here."

"The child was in to rule out MSUD but that came back negative. The baby has been spitting up a lot. She didn't seem to care for our regular soy formula."

"Have you tried holding her upright and rocking her for thirty minutes after her feedings instead of laying her down afterward? I once knew a baby with spit-up problems and that worked wonders."

"Funny you should say that. The social worker on the case came in a few minutes ago with the same suggestion."

Miriam stepped forward enough to see Hannah was sleeping quietly. Her color was pink and she looked perfect. "Can I sneak a peek at her?"

"I'm afraid not. Hospital policy and all that."

Miriam took a step back. "Sure. Thanks for letting me look around your unit."

Miriam turned to leave. The young nurse quickly asked, "Don't you want to talk to the charge nurse?"

Miriam shook her head. "I need a full-time job, but I'm sure you'll find someone who likes to work with babies."

She went out the door, gestured to Nick to follow her. He said, "If you want to take up police work, I can get you a recommendation."

"No, I'm happy being a nurse. We should get back to Mother."

"I'm going to stop and check on Mary Smith. I want to find out if I can talk to her soon. I'll catch you later." To Miriam's delight, he pressed a kiss on her lips. The thrill was over all too quickly when he pulled away. She longed for more.

She took the elevator back to her mother's floor. When she walked into her mother's room, she found Ada trying to get out of bed. Miriam rushed to help her.

"Mom, you should call for help before you get up."

"I called and I called, but no one came."

"I'm sorry, I went to see Hannah for a few minutes."

Her mother gave her a puzzled look. "Who is Hannah?"

"The baby that was left on our doorstep."

"Mark's baby?"

Miriam's heart sank to her feet. How had her mother learned about Mark's child? "No, Mother, it wasn't Mark's child. His baby was never born. His *Englisch* mother didn't want him."

Ada sighed heavily. "Have you been to plant flowers on Mark's grave? I wish you would. I can't go home until that is done."

Before Miriam could reply, her mother's eyes rolled back in her head and she collapsed into Miriam's arms.

Yelling for help, Miriam lowered her mother to the floor. A quick check of her pulse showed she was still alive. Relief flooded Miriam, but it was quickly thrust aside as the room filled with people. Miriam repeated what had happened to five different people including the nurses, a new resident and finally her mother's doctor.

He reviewed Ada's chart and listened to her heart for a long while before he turned to Miriam. "Her blood pressure is too low at the moment. I believe that's what caused her to faint. We're having so much trouble getting this medication regulated that I'm going to try her on something else. I know this is frustrating for you."

"*Scary* is the word I would use." Low blood pressure meant a sluggish flow of blood through the brain. That would account for her mother's confusion. Still, her mother's words haunted her. "I can't go home until that is done."

Had she meant home as in the farm, or home as in her heavenly home?

The thought chilled Miriam. It was time, long past time, for her to face her mistakes and admit them.

She left word with the nursing staff to call her if her mother's condition changed. In the hospital parking lot, she got in her car and headed toward the other side of town. It wasn't long before she was in the country she recognized from her childhood.

The highway wound through low hills and past pristine farms. Everywhere, signs of spring were turning the landscape green. In the pastures, tiny black-and-white calves frolicked together while their mothers grazed nearby.

After ten minutes, she reached the fork in the road that led to a small Amish cemetery.

She pulled her car to a stop beside the whiteboard fence that surrounded the property. For a long time she sat in the car not moving. It was the first time she had been back to visit Mark's grave since his funeral.

Opening the car door, she stepped out into the bright sunshine. The smell of new grass brought back memories from her childhood. With barely a thought, she kicked off her sneakers and stepped barefoot into a thick, cool green carpet.

Like all Amish children, she had spent her childhood barefoot. Not until frost hardened the ground each fall had she and Mark put on shoes. It felt right to visit him barefoot.

She made her way between the rows of nearly identical white headstones to his gravesite. When she came upon his name, tears welled up without warning as emotion choked her throat. With a moan, she sank to her knees and covered her face with her hands.

"I'm so sorry," she wailed as she rocked back and forth with grief. "I'd change it all if I could. I'm so sorry."

She had no idea how long she knelt there, but finally her sobs subsided. Weak and spent, she put her hand on the face of his marker. Would he forgive her? As she gazed at the stone, she brushed aside a small bit of moss growing on the edge of the stone. The clump fell to the grass and exposed something glittery. Reaching down, she picked up a silver star made of foil.

Instantly she knew where she had seen one before. Nick made one every time he put a piece of gum in his mouth.

Chapter Fourteen

Miriam spread the thick grass aside and saw more silver stars. Dozens of them lay around Mark's tombstone. Some were bright and new, others were old and dull, still others were mere flakes, having disintegrated from their time out in the elements.

"I started leaving them when I made sheriff."

Startled, she twisted around to see Nick standing behind her. She hadn't heard him approach.

Stepping forward, he laid a new star on the headstone. The breeze quickly blew it into the grass. "I put one out every time I come to visit."

Miriam rubbed at her tearstained face. "You've been here a lot."

"I have." He thrust his hands into the front pockets of his jeans. His shoulders were rolled forward as if he was expecting a blow across his back.

Was he waiting for her to say something? What words could convey the depth of what she was feeling? She looked up at his face. His hat cast a shadow across his eyes.

So much heartache. So much pain. Where is it all to end, Lord?

She knew the answer. It had to end with her. It was time for her confession. It was time to start healing. It might not happen today, or even tomorrow, but unless she spoke now, true healing would never happen for her.

"I'm glad you've come to his grave. I never could." She placed the star she held in her hand on her brother's stone. The wind died away and the star remained in place.

Nick squatted on his heels beside her. "Why haven't you come, Miriam? You were closer to him than anyone."

Sighing, she gripped her hands together until they ached.

Now or never. It was now or never.

"Because it was my foolish jealousy that led to his death and to the death of his child."

Nick's hand closed over her arm in a viselike grip. "What do you mean? What child?"

She looked into Nick's eyes. "Did you know he was in love with an *Englisch* girl?"

"No."

"All my life I thought I knew what I wanted,

Nick. I wanted to grow old as a member of the Amish community. I thought Mark wanted the same thing. From the time we were little we talked about the day we would be baptized into the faith. That all changed the day *she* came into his life."

"Who was she?" Nick asked. He eased his grip on her arm but didn't take his hand away.

"A girl who lived in Millersburg. Her name was Natalie Perry. I don't know how they met— he never told me that. He stopped telling me almost everything after they began going out. What he did talk about was leaving the faith."

"Miriam, it's not unusual for young Amish men and women to have their doubts."

She shook her head. "You don't understand, Nick. I don't think he had any doubts at all. I was so mad at them, both of them, for disrupting our lives."

"That's understandable."

She shrugged off his hand and rose to her feet. "Maybe, but what happened that last day was inexcusable."

Walking to the fence, she braced her hands on the white-painted boards, feeling the roughness of the planks against her skin. She couldn't face Nick or her brother's memory.

"I've already said I'm sorry a hundred times, Miriam. How many more ways can I say it?"

The anguish in his broken voice made her turn around. He stared at her with regret and pain etched in every feature.

Closing her eyes, she blocked the vision of yet one more life she'd damaged. "I wasn't talking about you, Nick. I was talking about what I did that forced Mark to steal a car and drive to his death."

Nick wasn't sure that he had heard Miriam correctly. "I don't understand. Are you saying that it wasn't a joy ride?"

She shook her head. "He was desperately trying to save his child's life."

"You keep talking about a child. What child?"

"Mark's unborn child. I promise you that I wouldn't have interfered if I had known about the baby."

He wanted to grab her and shake the truth out of her. All these years, he'd wrestled with the reason for Mark's behavior. It had never made sense. His death had been so meaningless. Nick forced himself to remain calm. "Tell me what happened."

"I know now that he must've loved her deeply, but he loved our family, too. I argued with him over and over that it was a mistake to go out into the world with her. I threatened to tell our parents and the bishop about them if he continued seeing her. Mark knew our family would be shunned if he ran off. I made him see he would break our parents' hearts—my heart, too. I convinced him it was God's will that he stay away from her."

Nick had been close to the Kauffman twins when they were all teenagers, but he had stayed away when he realized his feelings for Miriam went beyond friendship. Maybe, if he had hidden his own feelings better, Mark might have confided in him.

"Mark didn't see her for several weeks. The day before he died, she came to the farm. Mark had gone to visit some family with our parents. I could see Natalie was distraught, but I didn't have any sympathy for her. She had come close to destroying our family."

Miriam folded her arms across her chest and shivered. "Natalie told me her family was leaving the next day. She scrawled a note for Mark and thrust it into my hands. She begged me to give it to him as soon as possible."

"And did you?"

Tears ran unchecked down Miriam's face. "If only I had."

"Do you know what was in the note?"

"I gave it to him the next evening after supper. His face turned white when he read it. The look in his eyes frightened me to death. He dropped the note and ran out of the house. That was the last time I saw him alive."

"You said he dropped the note. You read it, didn't you, Miriam? Tell me what it said."

"It said she had just found out that she was pregnant and she didn't want the baby. I think her exact words were, 'I can't go through this alone. If you love me, come for me. I'll be waiting at the train station until nine o'clock. If you don't come, I will know you have made your decision, and I will have made mine. I'm not going to have this baby without you.'"

Miriam covered her face with her hands. "She was going to get rid of Mark's baby. That's why he stole our neighbor's car and wouldn't stop when you came after him. He was desperate to reach Natalie before she left town. The terrible accident was all because of me."

Miriam pressed a hand to her mouth and moaned. Her legs folded and she sank toward the ground. Nick caught her and held her against his chest as she cried.

Nick led Miriam to a small bench beside the caretaker's shed and sat beside her, holding her close as he'd always dreamed of doing. When her crying slowed, he lifted her tear-streaked face with a finger beneath her chin.

"Miriam, you can't keep blaming yourself for a mistake, no matter how serious you believe it is. We are human. We all make mistakes. Some of those mistakes have terrible consequences, but you have to forgive yourself. I know you thought you were protecting your brother."

She nodded. "I stopped seeing you because of my faith. I thought Mark should be able to do the same. I was jealous that his love for her was stronger than mine for you."

Nick pulled her close again. "I believe that Mark forgave you. He had to know you'd never willingly harm him or anyone. He was your brother. He loved you."

"I believe he has forgiven me, too. But can you forgive me? I let you carry the blame when I was the cause of it all. I'm so sorry for the harsh things I said and for the way I treated you."

"Of course I forgive you. Now that I understand Mark's motives for trying to outrun me it all makes sense. I respect what he was trying to do."

She cupped his face with her hand. "I'm glad I have given you some peace."

He turned his face to kiss the palm of her hand. "You have given me much more than peace. You've given me back one of the best friends I ever had. You."

And now he was going to give back pain.

Taking her hand, he held it between his palms. "Miriam, I have something I need to tell you. We got the DNA report back. I know who Hannah's mother is."

Her eyes widened. "Are you sure?"

"Yes, her mother is the young woman who tried to commit suicide. Her name is Mary Smith, but we think it's not her real name. The father has skipped town, but we're looking for him. There's a good possibility that he never knew Mary gave the baby away."

"But why would she do it?"

"The doctor feels she may be suffering from a case of postpartum psychosis. If so, she wasn't responsible for what she did. She may not even be aware of what she did. With treatment, she can recover and be a good mother."

Miriam's eyes softened. "I know that you love Hannah, too. I can only imagine how hard this must be for you."

"I appreciate that you understand. We can hope and pray for her, but little else."

"Life is so unfair."

"Amen to that."

She drew back a little. "How did you know where to find me?"

"I stopped by the hospital and your mother told me you'd come here."

"Mother told you? I never told her I was coming here."

"Then she made a good guess. Or maybe she knows you better than you think."

Worry creased Miriam's brows. "I need to tell her about Mark and his baby."

"It can wait until she is stronger."

"I guess you're right about that. Now that I've told you, it's as if the weight of the world has been taken off my shoulders." Her smile was bright and genuine.

"I'm glad." He wanted to know where he stood in her life now, but he sensed it wasn't the time for such questions. It was a time for healing. What Miriam needed was a supportive friend and he could be that.

He asked, "Are you okay to drive back to town?"

"I am. I don't want mother to start worrying."

"She seemed fine when I was there. She was eating a piece of peanut butter toast."

"Are you kidding me? She passed out cold this morning and scared me out of three years of my life."

"Like I said, she's a strong woman. You are, too, by the way. I hope you know that." He loved her strength and so much more about her. He prayed he'd have the chance to tell her exactly how he felt one day soon.

* * *

Miriam stared into Nick's eyes. She read more than friendship in their blue depths, but was she fooling herself?

He rose to his feet and offered her a hand up. She took it, cherishing the warmth that flowed from his hand to hers. He was a very special man, and she was going to do her level best to make up for the pain she'd caused.

He held her hand a moment longer than he needed to. "I'll let you know if I find out anything else about Hannah's father."

"It's an open case? I thought you couldn't talk about those."

"You've been involved from the beginning. I'll make an exception for you."

"Thanks. I guess I should get back."

"I've got to leave. Why don't you stay a little longer and visit with your brother? I think you need that."

"I think you're right. I'll see you later."

"Count on it." He tipped his hat and walked away.

Miriam followed his suggestion and spent a little time sitting by Mark's grave, talking about her life and about Hannah. In a way, she felt connected to him again—something that had been missing for far too long in her life.

When she returned to the hospital, she found

her mother sitting up in a chair and professing to feel great. It was a relief to see the new medication was agreeing with her.

"*Mamm,* how did you know I went to visit Mark's grave?"

"I couldn't think of any place else you would go without telling me if you weren't with Nick. And you've been talking a lot about your brother, lately."

Miriam frowned. "You are the one who has been mentioning him."

"Have I? I don't recall. I think the medicine has made me *narrisch*."

"You're not crazy, Mother. You've had some bad side effects, that's all."

"I wish I could go home. I'll get well much quicker there."

"If you do well on this new blood pressure medicine, I think you'll be home before you know it."

"How is Hannah? Have you heard anything about her?"

Miriam hesitated. Her mother looked so much better, but would the news of Hannah's situation cause a relapse? She chose to err on the side of caution. "Hannah is still here in the hospital and she is fine."

"I do miss that child. Who knew a person could fall in love with a baby so fast? I reckon

Nick will have to carry the baby bed back up to the attic. At least it got used for a little while. Perhaps I should sell it."

"That's something we can talk about later. For now, you need your rest."

"You need some rest, too, child. You look all done in."

"It's been an emotional day. Even that recliner isn't going to keep me awake tonight."

Later that night, Miriam woke with a start in the darkness of her mother's room. She had been dreaming about Hannah. She sat up in the chair to check her mother. Ada was sleeping peacefully. The monitor displaying her vital signs showed they were all normal.

Miriam sat back and closed her eyes, but she couldn't get Hannah out of her mind. There was no use trying to sleep when seeing the baby was the only thing that would make her feel better.

Miriam softly closed her mother's door as she left the room. It was after 2:00 a.m. and the hospital corridors were quiet. She took the elevator down one floor and turned left toward the nursery. As she approached the viewing window, she saw a young woman wearing a hospital gown standing in front of the glass. Her hair hung in a long blond braid down her back. She was barefoot and barely looked old enough to be a mother.

When she noticed Miriam approaching, she turned away quickly. Something in her posture made Miriam take a closer look. This wasn't a new mother happily looking in the window at her baby. This was a girl hoping not to be noticed.

The girl glanced over her shoulder. When she saw Miriam was watching her, she began walking away.

Miriam followed her and called out, "Wait a minute."

The girl walked faster. Miriam was practically running by the time she caught up with her. Reaching out, Miriam grasped her arm. The girl jerked away with a hiss of pain. It was then Miriam noticed the bandages on each of her wrists.

"I'm so sorry. *Ist es vay?*" Miriam asked with deep concern. The words meant, does it hurt? She wanted to know if what she suspected was true.

Shaking her head, the girl whispered, "Only a little."

"So you are Amish. I thought so. You must be Mary Smith, although Smith is hardly an Amish name. Why don't you tell me your real one?"

The girl froze, a look of fear in her eyes. She was so young. Little more than a child herself.

"Don't be afraid. I'm Miriam Kauffman. I'm sorry if I hurt you."

Staring at the floor, Mary remained silent.

"I saw you looking in the nursery window. She's in there, you know."

Mary raised her face a fraction. "Who?"

"Hannah. She ended up on my doorstep. Of course, you couldn't know that."

"I don't know anyone named Hannah. I don't know what you're talking about." Mary began backing away. "I don't want to get in trouble. I have to go."

"I'm talking about your baby, Mary. I know you told your boyfriend your baby was stillborn and that's why people think you tried to commit suicide, but that's not true."

"It is true—she's better off without me." Mary's voice was little more than a harsh whisper.

"I understand if you wanted her to have a better life, but I don't understand why you thought those Miller boys would make good parents. Between the two of them, they don't have enough sense to come in out of the rain."

Mary remained silent, but she didn't move away. Miriam began to hope she was getting through to her. "The only bright thing the twins did was leave the baby on my porch. Luckily, we found her before she got too cold."

"She shouldn't have been cold. I wrapped her in a quilt."

Miriam smiled. "The workmanship is quite lovely. Did you make it?"

"I stole it." The girl looked ready to bolt.

"With good reason." Miriam laid a hand on her shoulder in an effort to comfort her. The girl shrugged it off.

"I have to get back." She turned away and started to open the stairwell door.

"Don't you want to see her?" Miriam asked. "She's just down the hall in the nursery."

Mary froze. After a long moment, she closed her eyes. "I don't want to see her."

"Because you know if you do, you'll never have the strength to leave her again."

Mary's chin quivered but she didn't speak.

Miriam tried once more to comfort her. She gently brushed a strand of hair behind Mary's ear. Mary flinched, but allowed the touch. "I feel the same way about her. I had no idea how quickly I could fall in love with that little girl. I had no intention of loving her, but she has a way of looking at you that goes straight to your heart."

Mary looked up with angry eyes to glare at Miriam. "What do you want?"

"A long time ago, there was another young woman who didn't want to face being pregnant alone. I stopped her baby's father from helping her. I was never able to tell them how sorry I was and ask their forgiveness. Helping you and Hannah may just make up for that mistake."

"You can't help me."

"Oh, but I can. I do it all the time. I help young Amish people just like you to go out into the world."

"I've been out in the world. It's a bad place."

"Yes, it can be. Are you hungry?" Miriam glanced at her watch.

Mary looked perplexed, as if she couldn't follow Miriam's reasoning. "A little."

"Good. I believe the cafeteria is open for another half hour."

"I'm not supposed to leave the floor where my room is."

"You already have. I say we eat before we're caught. Sometimes it's better to beg forgiveness than to ask permission. I also need to check on my mother before I go. She's a patient here, too."

"What's wrong with her?" Mary glanced back toward the nursery as Miriam led her away.

"She has heart trouble. Having to give up Hannah brought on an attack. She's better now."

"Why didn't they let you keep the baby?"

Miriam pushed the elevator button. "*Englisch* law is a funny thing. It is designed with the best interest of the child at heart. They think Hannah belongs with her mother."

"But I gave her away. Doesn't that prove I'm a bad mother?"

The doors opened and Miriam stepped inside. "I guess that would depend on why you left her in an Amish buggy."

Mary didn't say anything, but she did enter the elevator.

Miriam breathed a sigh of relief. One small step at a time.

When the doors opened on her mother's floor, Miriam led the way, giving Mary a chance to follow or leave as she chose. At her mother's room, she opened the door softly to peek inside. To her surprise, the lights were on and her mother was sitting up in bed with a black knit shawl around her shoulders and her hair done up beneath her crisp white *kapp*.

She smiled at Miriam. "Come in. I've been waiting for you to come back. Esther Zook hired Samson Carter to bring her for a visit while you were gone yesterday. She brought us a shoofly pie and I feel like having a piece. How about you?"

She leaned forward to see behind Miriam. "Would your friend like some?"

Chapter Fifteen

Nick glanced from the tearstained face of the night nurse to the furious, red face of Dr. Palmer, the shrink in charge of Mary Smith, to the bulked-up security guard standing with his massive arms crossed. They were all trying to talk at once. Nick held up his hand to stop them. "You're saying she just walked out of this building and no one saw her leave?"

First he finds Hannah's mother and then he loses her again. This was starting out to be a bad day, and it was only four in the morning.

The nurse said quickly, "I can assure you, Sheriff, this has never happened before on our floor. The sitter staying with Mary Smith says she only nodded off for a few seconds. When she looked up, Mary was gone."

"She vanished from the entire hospital in seconds. I doubt that," Dr. Palmer grumbled.

"Either way, she's missing. What about Hannah?" Nick asked quickly.

The security officer said, "The nursery says she's fine. I called them first thing."

Relieved, Nick nodded. "I'll get an APB out on Mary Smith right away." He spoke into his radio and ordered the all points bulletin for a white female, approximately five foot tall with long blond hair, wearing a hospital gown when last seen.

There was little else he could do at the moment. He looked to Dr. Palmer. "Did you tell her that we have her baby?"

"I did."

"And what did she say?"

"Nothing. She still won't speak to me or to the staff."

"Any idea what would make her cut out? Was her boyfriend in to see her?"

The nurse shook her head. "No one has been to see her."

"That you know of," Dr. Palmer snipped.

Nick turned to the security officer. "Organize a search of the entire building, every broom closet and storage room. I want the security camera footage of the doors reviewed to see if she actually left."

"Will do." The burly man walked away, talking into his radio.

Nick said, "I'll be in the cardiac care unit if you need me." Miriam would want to know what had happened. She dealt with runaway teenagers all the time. Maybe she would have some insight that would be helpful in locating Mary Smith.

And maybe he just needed to see her again.

When he reached Ada's room, he paused outside the door. He didn't want to wake her or frighten her. He eased the door open to see if he could catch Miriam's attention. Instead of a dark room, he saw all the lights were on and the sound of Amish chatter filled the air. He stepped inside.

Ada was propped up in bed and involved in telling a story. Mary Smith sat cross-legged at the end of Ada's bed, a bright smile on her face. Miriam sat in a chair beside her mother and a nurse's aide sat in the recliner with a piece of pie on a paper plate.

Mary Smith saw him first. Her eyes went wide with fright. Miriam, seeing her distress, turned around. She waved at him. "Hi, Nick. Care for some shoofly pie? We have one piece left, but I'm afraid it's a small one."

Miriam turned back to Mary. "Don't worry, he's one of the good guys."

"Flattering as it is to hear you admit that, Miriam, can I ask what's going on here? Do you know that I have every officer in the county on the lookout for Ms. Smith?"

"Don't be silly, Nick. How could we know that? We've been in here since two-thirty."

"Having a party?"

Mary slid off the bed and spoke to Miriam in Pennsylvania Dutch. Miriam shook her head. The nurse's aide finished her last bite of pie and said, "I've got to get going. Thanks for the pie. It was great."

She had a faint German accent and Nick took her to be another ex-Amish. He stepped aside so she could slip out the door with a sheepish look on her face. He flipped the switch on his radio and canceled the APB, then he took a seat in the recliner. "What have I missed?"

Miriam brought him a thin slice of pie and said, "Mary Smith is really Mary Shetler, she's fifteen, not nineteen and Kevin isn't her husband or Hannah's father. Hannah's father is a married man in Canton. Hannah was working as a maid there and he seduced her. She ran away because she couldn't go back to her family. Her mother had passed away and her stepfather wasn't happy about having another mouth to feed. Mary hooked up with Kevin because he promised to take care of her, but he's into drugs and not a nice man. Mary thinks he's a drug runner. Each week he makes a trip to Canada."

Miriam paused to look over at Mary for confirmation. Mary nodded and fixed her gaze on her bare feet.

"That's a very interesting story. What I want to know is why Mary left her baby in the back of a buggy?"

Miriam scowled at him, but returned to her chair and waited for Mary to speak.

"Kevin wanted to sell the baby." Mary's voice trembled with fear.

"We told you he wasn't a nice man," Ada added. "That's all right, child. Tell your story."

Mary smiled at her and stood straighter. "He said we could get a lot of money for a baby like mine. I was scared he would go through with it and I wouldn't be able to stop him."

"He can't hurt either of you now," Ada assured her.

Mary nodded. "I took the baby and put her in the Amish buggy because I didn't want her to grow up in the *Englisch* world. I knew she would be safe with a good Amish family if I couldn't return. I left a note to tell them I'd be back for her. I needed time to get enough money to get away."

She fell silent and Nick said, "When they didn't return with her the next week, what happened?"

"I...I tried to be strong, but I knew I'd never

see her again. Not knowing where she was, if she was safe—I couldn't stand it."

"Did you slash your own wrists?" Miriam asked gently.

She nodded as tears ran down her cheeks.

Nick couldn't begin to understand what this girl had been through. He was only grateful that she had survived. One thing was certain. He'd make it his business to see that Kevin was brought to justice. "Will you testify to Kevin's intentions in a court of law? Can you give me the names of the people he was working with?"

Ada said, "We must forgive him. It is up to God to judge."

Miriam laid a hand on Mary's shoulder. "We do forgive, but we must also care for those who can't take care of themselves. Kevin may try to do this to another woman and her baby."

Mary looked at Nick and nodded. "I have names. I'll testify."

Miriam hugged her. "Now, you must grow strong because your baby is going to need you."

It took a long, hard week of police work, but Kevin Dunbar was finally behind bars in Nick's jail, and there wouldn't be any bail this time. It was with intense satisfaction that Nick closed and locked the cell door.

He returned to his office and started to pick

up the phone. He hadn't seen Miriam since her mother was dismissed from the hospital the day after Mary Shetler told her story. It had been far too long as far as he was concerned.

His secretary came in. "Sheriff, I took a message from Helen Benson. She wanted you to know that Hannah has been returned to the temporary custody of her mother. Hannah's case will remain open and the mother has to continue with her counseling but Helen is hopeful that Mary Shetler will be granted full custody in the future."

"Thanks. That's good news." It was for Mary and Hannah, but not for Miriam and Ada. Instead of the phone, he picked up his car keys. He'd rather deliver this news and his other news in person.

It took him thirty minutes to reach the turn-off to the Kauffman place. When he did, he saw Bishop Zook coming down the lane in his black buggy. Nick pulled to the side of the lane and waited.

When the bishop drew alongside, Nick rolled down his window. "Afternoon, Bishop. I hope all is well at the Kauffman place."

"All is better than well, Nicolas, for a lost sheep has returned to the fold. I performed a baptism this day. There is nothing but rejoicing in our hearts when such an event is brought about by God's mercy. I can't remember the last time I saw Ada so happy. I must get going, Sheriff, for I have cows that need milking and I have good news to spread." He tipped his hat and slapped the reins on his horse's rump. The mare trotted away, leaving Nick staring after the bishop in shock.

Miriam had been baptized into the Amish faith? Perhaps he should have seen it coming, but he hadn't. Not now, not when he was so certain they had a chance to be together.

He drove slowly up to the house thinking of all the lost chances he'd had to tell her how much he loved her.

He spotted Miriam hanging laundry on the clothesline beside the house. His heart turned over at the sight of her the way it always did and probably always would. He'd gained her forgiveness and opened the door for her to return to her Amish roots. He wanted to be happy for her, but he wasn't ready for that. The pain of loving her and losing her all over again was too new and two raw.

She waved when she spotted him and walked toward him with a laundry hamper balanced against one hip. She wore a dark blue dress with the long sleeves rolled up and an apron tied around her waist. A white kerchief covered her gorgeous hair. Her smile was bright and open, the way he remembered it when she was young. It was good to see her happy.

One of them deserved to be happy.

He got out of the car and waited with his hands thrust into the front pockets of his jeans.

"Nick, I was hoping to see you. I have so much to tell you that I hardly know where to begin." She stopped a few feet away. When he didn't respond, her smile faded, as if she was uncertain of her welcome.

He couldn't wish her happy when she was breaking his heart.

"I just stopped in to say goodbye and see how your mother is doing."

She frowned slightly. "What do you mean you stopped in to say goodbye?"

"There are some trout waiting patiently for me to toss my hand-tied flies close enough to bite." Maybe wading in the swirling waters might help him forget the way she felt in his arms. The way he wanted to kiss her, even now, when he knew it was wrong.

Relief filled her eyes. "I forgot, you have a vacation pending. You deserve some time off after all you have done for us."

"How is your mother?"

"The stent has helped enormously with her energy level and her new medication is working. She is happy as a lark and bossing everyone around again."

"I'm glad." He braced himself to say what he didn't want to say. "I'm glad, too, that you have found your heart's desire, Miriam. It means a lot to me to know that you are happy and at peace. I wish only the best for you."

"You sound so serious. Is something wrong?" Worry crept into her eyes once more.

Didn't she know how he felt? "Did you think this would be easy for me? I wish you had told me yourself instead of letting me hear it from the Bishop Zook."

"I thought you would be happy with my decision."

He took a deep breath and tried to disguise the hurt in his voice. "I will try to be happy for you, Miriam. Goodbye."

He turned back and started to open the car door. She dropped her laundry basket and stopped him by grabbing his wrist.

"Okay, I really didn't expect you would jump for joy, but I thought you'd be a little more enthusiastic. Tell me why you're unhappy about this?"

The warmth of her hand on his bare skin crumbled his defenses. "Do you really need to ask that?"

She stepped closer. "Apparently I do. Talk to me, Nick."

He closed his eyes. "I have loved you since I was twenty years old. I have never stopped loving you. I kept silent back then because I knew how much your faith meant to you. I could not ask you to choose me over your relationship with God. After Mark's death, it was almost a relief to realize how much you hated me. It made it easier to stay away from you. I'm glad you have returned to the Amish life, Miriam, but it will never be easy for me to stay away from you."

He felt her hands cup his face. Years of pent-up longing broke free and tears squeezed out from beneath his lashes. "I love you so much, Miriam."

"And I love you, Nicolas Bradley. I don't know where you got the idea that I have returned to my Amish roots, but you are grossly mistaken. I have no plans to leave my *Englisch* life."

His eyes popped open and he focused on her face so close to his. "Bishop Zook said everyone, particularly your mother, is rejoicing because the lost lamb has been returned to the fold. I thought he was talking about you."

"He was not talking about me. He was talking about Mary Shetler. She is the one who has returned to the fold. Yes, my mother is happy because she has a new daughter and a new granddaughter to help rear. That's the news I wanted to tell you. Mary and Hannah have moved in with me and my mother."

Unable to contain his joy, Nick pulled Miriam against his chest in a crushing hug. "Oh, thank you, God, for taking pity on this man. Thank you, God."

Miriam pulled her arms free of his grip and then slipped them around his neck. "I thank God daily for bringing you back into my life. I have been so blessed." Rising up on tiptoe, she kissed him as he had dreamed she would one day.

When she drew away, he saw love glowing in her eyes and his heart expanded until he thought it would break, not with sorrow, but with joy.

She smiled at him and he knew he would never tire of seeing that smile. "Nick, I have cared deeply for you since I was a teenager, but I never realized that I loved you until the day I found you rocking and singing to Hannah on the front porch."

He still couldn't believe he was holding her in his arms. "I love you. I don't care when you fell in love with me, only that you did."

"I didn't think I deserved to find love. Now I know God wants all his children to love and be loved in return. So maybe what I need is a little more practice at loving you." She lifted her face inviting his kiss. He was all too happy to comply.

As his lips closed over hers, the world narrowed to the softness of her skin and the taste of her lips, the way they fit his perfectly. His pulse hammered in his ears. He never wanted to lose her again.

When she finally broke away, he pulled her head forward and tucked it against his neck. "I think you're getting the hang of it."

Miriam smiled, breathing in the wonderful scent that was uniquely Nick's own. Resting in his arms, she was happier than she had ever been in her life. She loved him, and he loved her in return. God was indeed good.

She couldn't resist teasing Nick a little more. "You're lucky I'm something of a perfectionist. I'll keep trying until I get it right."

"Oh, you have it right, sweetheart. But if you want to keep practicing, I'm going to be available for the next seventy years."

She pulled back to look up at him. "Careful, Sheriff, that sounded surprisingly like a proposal."

He cleared his throat and held her at arm's length. "I've always believed that good communication is the key to any relationship. So let me be clear about this. Miriam Kauffman, will you do me the honor of becoming my wife?"

She stared at him in stunned surprise. "Nick, are you serious?"

"I've never been more serious in my life. We have wasted enough time."

"Two weeks ago I didn't even like you."

"If you've come this far in two weeks, I can only imagine how good things will be in two months or two years. I understand that this was rather sudden because, believe me, I didn't come here intending to propose. So if you want some time to think it over, I understand completely, but I couldn't stop myself from offering you my heart. I thought I'd lost you."

"Yes."

He eyed her intently. "Yes, you want some time to think it over? Or yes, you will marry me?"

"In an effort to improve the communication in our relationship, let me be perfectly clear. Yes, Nicolas Bradley, I will marry you."

"Are you sure?"

"Are you trying to make me change my mind?"

He pulled her close once more. "Not at all, darling. I just can't believe that I've attained my heart's desire."

She snuggled closer. "I'm good at helping people discover what it is that they really want."

He chuckled and she felt the sound reverberate in his chest beneath her ear. She would never grow tired of being held in his arms. He lifted her hand and placed a kiss on her palm. "When?"

"When what?" she asked with dreamy happiness.

"When can we get married?"

From behind Miriam, Mary said, "It looks like it had better be soon."

Miriam twisted in Nick's hold but she didn't move out of his embrace. "I think I would enjoy a long engagement. What do you think, Nick?" She gave him a saucy glance.

"I will wait for as long as it takes. As long as it doesn't take more than two months."

"Two months!" Ada had come out onto the porch with Hannah in her arms.

Nick said, "I can take her off your hands faster if you need me to, Ada."

"Bah, no one can get ready for a wedding in two months. We shall need at least six months."

"Is that what you want?" Nick whispered into her ear. His warm breath sent a chill up anticipation sweeping across her body.

"I want to stay here, wrapped in your arms for the rest of my life."

"My thoughts exactly." He pressed a kiss on her temple. It was nice, but she wanted more. She turned and raised her face. His lips found hers and she gave herself over to the magic of his touch.

Hannah began to fuss. Ada said, "Enough with the kissy-kissy. The baby wants to be fed, and we have many plans to make. Come inside everyone."

Nick stopped kissing Miriam long enough to say, "We'll be along in a little bit, Ada. Your daughter and I have a lot of lost time to make up for."

Mary laughed and shook her head. She took Hannah from Ada's arms "Kids today, they never listen to their elders."

As she followed Ada back inside the house, Miriam gazed up at Nick. She would never grow tired of seeing the love shining in his eyes. "Before we get hitched, there is one thing you should know."

"Only one?"

"This is an important thing. I intend to adopt Mary. Both she and my mother are in favor of it. That way, if anything happens to my mother, or to me, Mary and Hannah will always have a place to live."

Nick raised one hand to rub his jaw. "You mean in addition to getting a bride, I'm also going to be getting a teenage daughter—with the baby."

"That's right, Grandpa."

He groaned. "Grandpa? I thought I'd have twenty-five or thirty years before I got stuck with that label."

"Well?"

"Well what?" he asked as he pulled her close and settled her against his hip.

"We come as a package deal. Take all of us or take none of us."

He kissed the tip of her nose. "You drive a hard bargain, Miriam Kauffman. I'll do it as long as you include Bella in the deal."

"Done." She smiled at him with all the love in her heart.

"What do you think Mark would say about this?" His question held an odd edge.

"I think Mark is glad. He loved both of us."

"How do you think your mother would feel about having an English grandchild?"

Miriam rolled her eyes. "You are getting a little ahead of yourself, Sheriff. You haven't walked down the aisle with me yet."

"I wasn't talking about us. I've been debating whether to tell you this or not, but I think I should. I did some digging, and I found Mark's girlfriend, Natalie Perry. She lives in St. Louis now, with her eight-year-old son."

Miriam blinked hard. Had she heard Nick right? "She kept Mark's baby?"

"Yes, she did."

"Nick, that is wonderful. Oh, my goodness, how I agonized over the thought that I was responsible for two deaths. I'm so glad."

"I knew you would be—that's why I came here today. I wanted to give you some good news, and to tell you Kevin Dunbar has been arrested. Will you tell your mother about Mark's child?"

"I have already told her about my part in Mark's death. I told her the reason he was on the road that night. She will be as thrilled as I am that Natalie kept the baby. Do you think there's any chance that we could meet her and see him? Do you know his name?"

"His name is Mark."

Tears welled up in her eyes as words failed her. Nick slipped a finger beneath her chin and tipped her face up. "Please, don't cry."

"They are happy tears, Nick. Come inside and give *Mamm* the news."

She started toward the door, but he caught her hand and pulled her back. "Not so fast. We have unfinished business."

She grinned at him. "What business would that be?"

"You haven't said *when* you will marry me. I'm not leaving this spot until I have an answer."

Miriam wrapped her arms around his neck. "In that case, we could be here all night."

"I'm in favor of that." He lowered his head. Miriam had a moment to thank God for His mercy and goodness before Nick's kiss made her forget everything but the wonder of his love.

* * * * *

Dear Reader,

I hope that you enjoyed *A Home for Hannah*. So many of you have asked me to tell Nick's story. I'm happy to oblige. He and Miriam had a rocky relationship, but God has a plan for us all, even when we can't see it.

Coming next will be another story about Hope Springs. In December, look for *A Hope Springs Christmas*. Sarah Wyse, the Amish widow who works in the fabric store, is about to discover she has a knack for matchmaking. But does she know that love has been living next door to her for years?

Shy buggy maker Levi Beachy is in need of a wife, but he doesn't know it. It's up to his sister and his mischief-making twin brothers to find one for him. Can Sarah help? Yes, she can, but finding the perfect wife for Levi may just involve finding the perfect mate for herself, too.

Love springs eternal in Hope Springs.

Many blessings to you and yours.

Patricia Davids

Questions For Discussion

1. Miriam could not forgive Nick for his part in her brother's death. Without forgiveness there can be no healing. How can we learn to forgive the hurts of others?

2. Do you think Miriam was right when she said it is easy to say you have forgiven someone when actually meaning it is much harder? Why or why not?

3. Why do you read Amish fiction? What is the attraction?

4. At what point did you begin to see Nick was the man Miriam might love again?

5. I love reunion stories. How did this reunion story differ from others that you have read?

6. What new information, if any, did you learn about the Amish in this story?

7. Providing foster care is a calling. Have you considered fostering a child or pet? Why or why not?

8. Bella makes a good nanny dog. Have you had a dog that was good with kids? What was his or her name? Share about your pet.

9. What concept that the Amish embrace do you find the hardest to understand? Shunning? No phones? No electricity? Why?

10. Have you visited an Amish community? What did you enjoy about it? What did you find disappointing about it?

11. Miriam felt a lifetime of good works might make up for the one mistake she made in not giving her brother the note from his girlfriend. Can good works make up for mistakes? In our eyes? In God's eyes?

12. Nick was Miriam's first love. Do you remember your first love? Why didn't it work out? Or did it?

13. Do you think Nick and Miriam can work out a happy future with two demanding careers? Why? Why not?

14. Are you likely to read more Amish romances?

15. Is there someone you need to forgive?

LARGER-PRINT BOOKS!

GET 2 FREE
LARGER-PRINT NOVELS
PLUS 2 FREE
MYSTERY GIFTS

Love Inspired

Larger-print novels are now available...

Love Inspired

SUSPENSE

RIVETING INSPIRATIONAL ROMANCE

Watch for our series of edge-
of-your-seat suspense novels.
These contemporary tales
of intrigue and romance
feature Christian characters
facing challenges to their faith...
and their lives!

**AVAILABLE IN REGULAR
& LARGER-PRINT FORMATS**

For exciting stories that reflect traditional values,
visit:
www.ReaderService.com